SAFE WITH YOU

BOOK 1 IN THE WINTER'S ROSE SERIES

LIZZIE JAMES

Published by Lizzie James 2020

Edited by Eleanor Lloyd-Jones at Schmidt Author Services

Formatted by Phoenix Book Promo

Cover Design by Eleanor Lloyd-Jones at Schmidt Designs

Cover Models: Lance Jones & Cassia Brightmore

To my mother, Susan
Thank you for teaching me how to be strong

Prologue

orking for myself, I always had one rule: work hard, play harder and don't ever be afraid to reach higher. That was the way that I lived my life... until she came along. She tipped my world upside down, shook it until there was nothing left in its right place. She came in like a tornado and destroyed it all.

Looking back, I realised how much of a fool I was, but at the time, I was a happy fool. If I could go back and change anything, the scary part is, I don't think I'd change a thing.

And that was the part that wrecked me.

CHAPTER
One

Charlie

$\mathscr{B}$eing an only child I had learned from a young age that the only person you could count on was yourself. If you couldn't drag your arse from the hole that you had fallen into, you were pretty much screwed. There were no prince charmings or fairy godmothers. Not in my life.

Walking into work, I smiled at my colleagues as I made my way to my desk. From my first day working at this corporation, I had learned that a smile could get you through any door. It's why I always made sure to appear as if I had my shit together. Even when I didn't.

I took a seat at my cubicle and plugged my headset in. I worked for a large call centre that offered technical support to several other large companies. I worked in the broadband and software development department, and I loved my job. Some people assumed that you had to be intelligent to be technical but really, you just had to have an interest in how things operated.

It was my dream to be a baker, though—to have my very own shop and sell delicious, gorgeous treats.

From a young age, my mother told me I was always taking things apart and then putting them back together again. She said I had a curiosity to learn how things worked. Working here, it was my goal to make it to team leader level. Well, that was until 'that' day happened.

"Charlotte, can I see you in my office, please?"

I looked up and smiled at Suzie. She was my line manager and someone that I always thought liked me.

"Of course." I stood and removed my headset before following her to her office. "Is there a problem?" I asked, taking a seat in one of the chairs facing her rather large oak desk.

She took her seat behind it before she released a gentle sigh. "I'm afraid I have some bad news, Charlotte."

I really hated it when they called me by my full name. I preferred Charlie.

"I'm sorry, but I am going to have to let you go."

Well, that was blunt. "Can I ask why?" I asked. "I thought that I was doing well and I—"

She held her hand up. "This isn't personal,

Charlotte. We have had to cut some posts and I'm very sorry to report that yours is one of them. If I could keep you, I would, but I just can't. I'm sorry."

She didn't look sorry. If anything, she looked bored.

I nodded and slowly stood. I leaned across the desk and shook her hand before leaving her office. I opened the door and froze when a woman came running past me in floods of tears. I guessed she was one of the sacked.

I went to my desk and grabbed my handbag, not even bothering to finish the rest of my shift. I know it would have been the mature thing to do but I just couldn't be bothered. I was gutted and right then, all I wanted to do was to go home and sulk.

Walking through the streets of London, I tried not to get too upset but I couldn't help it. If I didn't get another job—and soon—it would be likely that I'd have to go back to Wales. I really didn't want to think of doing that because I loved London. London had it all: museums, bookshops, tourism, shows... No matter where you came from, there was something for everyone.

Going back to Wales would feel like a step backwards.

After taking a train through several tube stops, I was relieved to finally be home. Sliding the key into the lock, I toed my shoes off, making sure to be extra quiet. I lived with my roommate, Addie, who was a dancer at a burlesque club. She was single and had a bigger shoe obsession than a supermodel. Addie usually didn't get in until gone two am, so I always tried to be extra quiet in the mornings. She'd usually wake up around noon looking refreshed as ever. Deciding to hide in my bedroom until then, I crawled into bed and snuggled up, trying to block out my morning.

Getting sacked was an experience I didn't think I was going to get over anytime soon.

I closed my eyes, determined to get some sleep until Addie woke up when I was jostled from the side by her tiny body joining me in bed.

"How come you're home?" she asked. Addie didn't have an inside voice. She only knew one volume and that was loud.

"I got fired," I admitted sulkily.

"Oh, Charlie!" She wrapped her arms around me and hugged me from behind. "I'm so sorry." She kissed the side of my head and squeezed me tighter. "What are you going to do now?"

"I don't know, Addie." I reached down and held her hand. "I don't want to go back to Wales."

She was shaking her head before I had even finished talking. "That won't happen." She stood and came dancing around to my side. "I have an idea. Let's go out tonight." She was being too enthusiastic.

I pulled the blanket over my head, attempting to hide from her. "I just want to hide."

She yanked the blankets down and cocked her eyebrow at me. "Come on! I have an idea. Come to Alex's with me for a few drinks before my shift tonight."

"I thought I would check the job advertisements first and I…"

This time she raised both her eyebrows at me. "And you what?" she asked in a sweet tone. "Before I try and push you on to the hot sexy barman that has been interested in you since the moment he saw you?"

"No, he isn't!" I denied, feeling embarrassed. I rolled my eyes at her. "It's just…" I looked at the floor, not really sure how to bring it up. How did I tell my best friend that things had been strange since David?

David was my boyfriend—well, ex-boyfriend rather. I'd met him when I first moved to London. He was an engineer and we had been happy. We were together for about six months and at the time, I'd thought it was a perfect six months. Well, as perfect as we could have been until I'd walked in on him screwing his receptionist on his desk. The relationship had quickly ended for me, but he was having trouble letting go. In the last couple of weeks, I had seen him hanging around my office building during his lunch hour.

I looked back up at her. "I've just never been sacked and I…"

She rolled her eyes and took a seat next to me. She reached over and placed her hand on mine. "It's David, isn't it?" She dipped her head to look at me. "You haven't been the same since you guys ended and…" She sighed. "I just want you to see that you're better off without him."

"I know that." I smiled at her, trying to ease the worry I could see in her eyes. "I've just never been fired before. Or cheated on." I hated that tears leaked out over my eyes. I should have been stronger than this.

She pulled me into her side and stroked the hair back from my face. "It's okay, sweetie. It's going to be okay." She rocked me for a few moments until my tears stopped. "Now, how about we go out tonight, have a few drinks, maybe some laughs and we can handle the job vacancies tomorrow. And maybe we can perv on a sexy bartender or two." She held her hand out to me. "Deal?"

I grasped her hand and giggled when she yanked me to my feet. "You win." I allowed her to drag me from my room and into the kitchen where I cooked us some lunch and she filled me in on all the drama I had missed on the Italian soap drama she had recently become obsessed with.

---

*S*itting at a high table in Alex's bar with Addie, I laughed. We'd had a few cocktails and it was so nice to just hang out together—just me and her. I watched Addie stretching her legs down to reach the floor. We were sitting on tall bar stools and she was way too short.

She grabbed her jacket and slid her arms through. "Do you want me to walk you home?"

"No, I'm okay." I looked over to the bar and saw that Alex was still working. "I think I'll hang out here for a bit longer and then head home."

She grinned at me before she pulled me into a hug. "Go sit at the bar." She gave me a wink. "Alex hasn't been able to take his eyes off of you all night." She gave me a little wave and left me, leaving for her shift at her club.

I gave a sneaky look over to the bar and cringed when I saw Alex standing there. He was cleaning a glass and was staring over at me. Before I could look away, he nodded his head at the empty stool at the bar. I drained the last of my cocktail and placed the glass down. I slid myself off the bar stool. I walked over, trying to keep my cool but I could feel the nerves creeping up my spine.

Alex was the owner of this bar, and he and I had never really hung out together. Any time I had ever seen him, I had always either been with Addie or David. He was over six feet tall and had gorgeous brown eyes and dark hair and always had stubble on his cheeks and his arms were inked with tribal designed tattoos. He was also sexy as hell.

"Hi." I greeted him with a small smile and placed my purse on the bar. "It's nice to see you, Alex."

His eyes trailed down to my chest where I had a bit of cleavage showing before making a slow pass back up to my face.

I was a little embarrassed with the way that he was staring at me. When I'd decided on my jeans and this low-cut top, I hadn't been imagining anyone looking at me the way that he was. Especially not him. I pulled my blonde hair forward to cover some of my cleavage and looked back to him.

"Take a seat, Charlotte." He nodded his head at the empty seat and placed his hands on top of the bar. "What can I get for you?" He gave me a sexy grin and I knew that I was probably blushing from it.

I lifted myself up into the chair and opened my purse. "I'll have a vodka and cranberry, please."

Before I could slide my cash across to him, he held his hand up.

"It's on me." He filled my glass and placed it on a bar mat in front of me. "You look a little down."

"I got fired today." I stirred the straw, mixing the cranberry juice in and took a sip.

"Are you going to go back home?" He raised his eyebrows at me. "Or are you going to look for another job?"

I nodded my head. "Addie is going to help me look

at the vacancies tomorrow. I don't really want to go back to Wales."

He nodded his head. "You, uh…" He scratched the back of his neck. "I have a spot next door if you want it."

My eyes shot up to his. "Next door?" Now I was confused.

"I own this building and the one next door. Addie spoke to me earlier and told me how you've always wanted to be a baker. To have your own place one day."

I widened my eyes at him. "Are you serious?" I shrieked in surprise.

He laughed. "You can pay me rent when you're up and running and see where we go from there. Maybe stock my menu with some tasty treats?" He grinned at me. "So, what do you say, Charlotte?"

I hated it when people called me Charlotte but when he said my name… It just made me want to climb him like a tree. I stared at him, trying to figure him out. He and I hadn't spoken much before this besides friendly chatter, and now here he was offering me a job —not just any job but my dream job.

"Why are you offering me this?" I asked. "I mean, I'm not…"

"I know how it feels," he said. "This place…" He waved his hand around to indicate the bar. "This place didn't happen overnight. I got here by asking for help when I needed it."

I looked at him, trying to imagine him asking for help. I couldn't see it, though. The man in front of me seemed so confident and sure of himself. It was difficult to imagine him ever being weak or vulnerable.

"Can I think about it?" I asked.

His face fell before he slowly nodded. "Sure." He pasted a fake smile on his face. "Take all the time you need." He walked away and headed toward some customers further down the bar, leaving me alone to my vodka and thoughts.

As I drained the last of my drink, I grabbed my purse and gave him a small wave and made my way to the exit. I couldn't help but look back at him, still remembering the way that his face dropped when I asked if I could think about his offer. I shook my head at myself when I saw he was being chatted up by some beautiful blonde woman who was now sitting in my seat. I don't know why I was disappointed. I'd never have a chance of keeping a guy like that interested.

I turned left and made my way down the street. As I got closer to my building with only one small block left to go, I looked over my shoulder, hating the feeling of eyes on me. It was a stupid feeling. David had really messed my head up with his hanging outside my workplace, and now I felt like his eyes were on me whenever I was out of my building on my own.

Walking through the main door, I let out a sigh of relief when it clicked shut behind me. David had never meant to be mean or nasty to me when we'd been together, but being followed made me feel paranoid. Being watched was never a nice feeling.

After locking the door to my apartment, I toed off my shoes and changed into my pyjamas before crawling into bed. The way that I was feeling right now, I hoped that tomorrow I would feel better.

I closed my eyes and drifted away to the thought of seductive, chocolate brown eyes and the promise of a better world.

CHAPTER Two

Alex

That woman killed me. She had no idea how beautiful she was and no clue how much she owned the room when she was in it. She was sexy without even trying.

I'd first met Charlotte when she'd been in a relationship with that knob, David. That fucker had had no idea how lucky he was to have a stunner like her in his life, and it had made me so fucking mad when I would see him sneaking around behind her back with other women. She hadn't had a clue and it aggravated me that I'd never said anything to her, but I'd known that if I had told her, she would freak.

I'd been afraid that she wouldn't believe me.

I'd felt I only had one chance with Charlotte, and I

wasn't going to fuck it up on a wanker like David. She'd found out the truth without me, and I was glad for it. She deserved more than to be cheated on.

Watching her across the room with Addie had been fucking hell. I was jealous as fuck that Addie had been the one making her laugh. I wanted to be the one who made her laugh. I didn't do jealousy. I was a confident man and the fact that this little woman had me feeling like this made my blood boil. She had no idea how I felt about her and I needed that to change.

I wanted her, and I usually got what I wanted.

I'd hated the look on her face when I'd offered her my place next door. I'd been able to see the shutters coming down. She didn't trust me. After David, she probably didn't trust *any* man.

I was determined to change that.

It was an hour before closing, and I was hoping for a quiet finish, but luck wasn't on my side. Addie came sauntering through my door with a wicked smile on her face.

"Hi, handsome." She took the seat that her roommate had occupied hours earlier, resting her elbows on top. "So, how did it go with Charlie?"

"Do you pimp your roommates out often, Addie?" I raised my eyebrows at her, waiting on a response.

"Please!" She rolled her eyes at me. "She'll thank me one day. Besides, I know you're a good guy."

"And what idiot told you that?" I uncapped a bottle

of Budweiser and took a swig from it. "I offered her the place next door."

"What did she say?" she asked. Her eyes sparkled a little. "Did she take it?"

"No." I shook my head. "She said she wanted to think about it."

Her shoulders slumped a little before she straightened up. "Come around to mine for breakfast in the morning. Give her a reason to say yes." She turned to the side and blew me a kiss. "I'll see you around." She walked out the door, leaving me to close up.

After locking up, I made my way upstairs to my apartment, checking the windows before taking a shower. After a long day of being stuck behind the bar, I felt dirty and sweaty.

I couldn't get Addie's words out of my head.

"Give her a reason to say yes."

What the fuck could I say? Convincing a woman to my way of thinking wasn't exactly one of my skills. There was a reason I was a bachelor at the end of the day. Being with a woman for more than one night wasn't a part of my plan, but Charlotte...

Fuck me, she was *THE* girl. She was smart, beautiful, sexy, kind and sweet as hell. She was pure and light and too damn good for me.

Climbing into bed, I resigned myself to going over

in the morning with donuts and attempt to sell my offer in a positive light. It was a business arrangement, and I had a feeling that she would be more than comfortable keeping it as such.

Her head was fucked, and if I took what I wanted from her, it would be even more fucked up.

My darkness—my past—would just swallow her light.

S tanding outside her apartment, I knocked on her door. I didn't like how tense I was feeling. Alexander Winters didn't fucking do tense.

The door swung open, what was waiting for me on the other side of the door surprising the fuck out of me. Charlotte stood there in only a pair of shorts and a sports bra.

Fuck me, she was stunning.

"Uh, Alex." A blush took over her cheeks. She was mortified. She crossed her arms over her chest attempting to cover herself. "What do you…? Can I help you?" She raised her eyebrows, waiting.

"Addie came by the bar last night and asked me to come by?" I was going to kill Addie. Charlotte didn't have a clue about me coming over.

"Oh!" She took a step back. "Please, come in. Addie isn't here at the moment but…"

"Actually…" I walked through her door and stepped to the side so she could close it. "I've brought my business plan over," I said, holding the folder up in my hand. "I thought we could discuss my offer from last night. I even brought donuts." I held the box out to her, smiling when she took it.

"You have a good selection here," she said, peeking into the box. She turned and led me to her kitchen. "You even have chocolate and jelly ones!"

I was unable to keep my eyes off how perky her little arse looked in those shorts. Before I could look up, she spun around, catching me checking her out. She blushed and quickly grabbed her hoodie that was on the back of the chair at the table and quickly pulled it over herself, hiding her delectable body from my view.

"Would you like a coffee?" She turned back to the worktop, avoiding my gaze. "We have tea or…"

"Coffee is good, thanks." I pulled a seat out at her table, trying not to make things worse by staring at her arse again. "Black with two sugars, please."

She quickly made us some coffee and placed the box of donuts on the table.

"Help yourself." She grabbed a chocolate one and took a bite. "That's so good." She moaned at the taste.

"You're a chocolate addict." I grinned at her.

"The biggest." Her eyes flicked down to the folder in front of me as she reached up to wipe the chocolate smudged on the corner of her lips. "So, what is it you wanted to talk about?"

"Right." I nodded my head and put my coffee to the side. "So, the building next to me has had all its necessary testing. The emergency lighting is up to code and a gas safety certification was carried out last week. It passed with flying colours."

"Okay." Her eyes flicked down to the certificates in the file before coming back up to me.

"I originally bought the building as I was planning to extend the bar into a dance area but I decided against it." I don't know why the hell I was sitting there explaining myself. "Look, I understand you have other things going on in your life, but I was serious about leasing the place out to you."

"I don't know, Alex…" She took a sip of her coffee. "What if I mess it up? What if it doesn't…?"

"You won't mess it up. I'm sorry if this sounds harsh but you're never going to know if you don't try." I stared at her for a few moments before I spoke again. "If you're worried about owing me anything, you wouldn't. This would be yours. I'd have no input."

"I guess I can use the redundancy money I'll be having in a couple of weeks to help me get set up until the doors open." She nibbled on her bottom lip before a beaming smile took over her face. "Okay. Let's do this." She held her hand out to mine and we slowly shook.

The door behind me opened and Addie's voice joined us. "What's going on? Ooh! Is that donuts?"

"I'm going to be a baker!" Charlotte shrieked. They both squealed and hugged each other tightly.

"I'll leave you ladies to celebrate." I began walking to the main door. "I look forward to seeing what you'll come up with, Miss Chase."

She giggled at me. "Maybe we can have a chat about that when I'm up and running."

"Sure." I reached into my pocket and tossed a key to her. "If you need anything else, you know where to find me." I winked at her, loving the blush that appeared on her face.

I left them to it and made my way down the block towards the bar. I looked back and froze when I saw who was hanging outside her building: her waste of space of a cheating ex was sitting on a bench, glaring in my direction. I turned around to walk back up and move him along but stopped when he got up and began walking in the other direction.

That fucker had a serious problem.

*I*t had been a few weeks since I had last spoken to Charlotte. I had seen her going past the bar enough times, carrying gadgets that she would need for her new venture. She'd already paid a month's rent to my accountant, and it looked like she was determined to have an opening date soon.

I really needed to make an effort to go and have a talk about her making some treats for the dessert menu.

"Still pining over that chick next door?" James took a seat at the bar. "Didn't think I'd ever see the day where *you'd* be tamed by one woman."

"What do you want?" I asked, ignoring his comments. "Your shift doesn't start for another hour."

"I thought I'd swing by and see if you wanted to get some lunch."

I shook my head. "I have paperwork to go over and then I'm going to…"

"Go and check on your obsession next door and see if you can find another detail of hers to stalk over?" He laughed. "Dude, just grow a pair and ask her out."

"I don't stalk," I quickly defended.

He cocked an eyebrow at me. He knew I was bullshitting.

"She just got out of a relationship, man, and do you remember? I don't do relationships."

"Who's saying it has to be a relationship?" He tapped his hand against the bar before giving me a one-handed salute and going past me in the direction of the staff room.

"I'll be back in a few," I called out. I quickly went through the exit, ignoring his mocking laugh.

Heading next door, I walked straight in without

knocking. I looked around and saw she already had several sets of tables and chairs arranged and had a worktop installed with several high-top chairs set up. She had obviously gotten the ball rolling and was eager to begin opening soon.

"What do you think?" She came out of the door that connected to her large kitchen at the back. "We're having an ice cream counter set up in the corner where customers can choose what flavour they would like with their waffles and pancakes."

"It sounds like you're almost ready." I chuckled when I saw she had a toffee sauce stain on her cheek.

"Oh no." She walked further into the room. "I need to do some test dishes first and finish getting the place ready."

"Dishes?" I asked. "For me?" I walked closer and took a seat at her worktop. "I was thinking we could have a meeting to discuss the dessert menu in the bar."

"Really?" She smiled at me before coming to a stop in front of me, with the worktop between us. "You'd trust me to be your official dessert supplier?" She said it mockingly, but I knew that she was teasing.

"Of course. I would need to test these samples myself," I joked. "For research purposes, of course."

She giggled. "Of course. I suppose I could do some test dishes and bring them by one night."

"Or I could come here? I could finish early one night and get James to watch the bar."

"Okay." She smiled at me. "That might be easier."

I reached over and rubbed my thumb along the toffee on her cheek. Her eyes widened at my actions and I couldn't stop myself from what I did next. I sucked the toffee off my thumb, humming at the taste. "That's sweet." I grinned at her and slid off my chair. "So, when do you want to do this tasting session?"

"Tomorrow night?" She fidgeted with her hands, linking her fingers together. "Around six? No! Seven!"

I chuckled at her babbling. "Sounds good." I smiled at her before giving her a wave. "I'll see you tomorrow, Charlotte."

"It's Charlie." She reached up and tucked a curl behind her ear. "I prefer for my friends to call me Charlie."

I nodded my head and exited her building.

Tomorrow with Charlie sounded fucking perfect.

CHAPTER
Three

Charlie

"That smells delicious!" Addie slid on to the stool that Alex had been occupying the previous day. "Can I have some?" She craned her neck to spy what was in the oven behind me.

"Absolutely not." I flicked my towel at her. "Those caramel bites are for Alex. I made extras for him to take away with him."

"You sound pretty sure of yourself there." She stared at me for a moment as a sneaky smile appeared on her face. "Are you blushing?"

"No!" I quickly defended. "No." I shook my head in denial before giving in and nodding my head. "Yes."

"Tell me everything!" She leaned forward on her elbows.

I rolled my eyes at how eager she sounded. "When he was here last night, I had some toffee sauce on my cheek and he… He wiped it off my cheek."

"And?" she demanded.

"He licked the sauce off his thumb."

We both burst into giggles.

"He's into you!" Addie reached across and took my hand in hers. "Do you like him?"

"Don't be silly, Addie! I mean, look at him. There's no way he would ever be interested in me. I'm a mess."

"No, you *were* a mess. When you were with that idiot of an ex, you weren't the same girl. He controlled you." She shook her head. "You could always do better than that fool. And…" She mock-swooned. "Alex is *so* much better."

"It's too soon, Addie. I don't think I'm ready for anything serious."

We were disturbed when the main door opened and in walked Alex. Addie looked back at me and raised her eyebrows.

"Who said it had to be serious?" She wiggled her eyebrows at me before she slid out of her seat. "Have fun guys! Don't do anything I wouldn't do." She winked at Alex as she passed, embarrassing me further.

"Am I too early?" Alex asked, taking a seat.

"Not at all." I turned around and grabbed my apron, tying it around my waist. "I just hope you enjoy what I made for you."

"I'm sure I will." He pointed his thumb over his shoulder. "Addie could have joined us if you…"

"No!"

He laughed at my outburst.

"I mean…" I rolled my eyes. "Addie can be a bit bossy."

"I noticed that." He looked past me. "So, what do you have for me first?"

I took a seat on the other side of the worktop next to Alex as I watched him pop another caramel bite into his mouth.

"So, out of all the desserts, which is your favourite?" I was eager to know if he'd enjoyed them.

"You expect me to pick just one?" He turned in his seat to face me. "If I had to pick one, I'd probably say the caramel bites." He reached for another and popped it in his mouth. "Your cheesecake and gateaux are very tasty as well."

"Well, I can't just fill your menu with caramel bites." I giggled. "You need to tell me what you want."

There went another caramel bite.

"How about you just give me a selection and we can build the menu from there?"

I shook my head at him. "Men can never make decisions." I grabbed the notepad and pen and began writing a list of desserts. "I think if we start with six or seven and we can have around four as a mini selection. Maybe put some muffins, bakewells and brownies on there as well?" I looked up at him to see if he agreed with me.

"That sounds good to me. I'll get the menu updated."

I tore it from the notepad and slid the list across to him. "Just let me know when you'd like me to start and we can…"

"Next week?" He folded the note up and put it in his jean pocket. "It could be a good test run for you."

"Okay. Feeling the pressure now." I slid down from my stool and picked the empty dishes up. "I'll just get your caramel bites for you."

"You made me extra?" he asked. He sounded surprised.

"I did." I went into the kitchen and felt him follow me.

"Wow!" He looked at all of my kitchen gadgets laid out in their spaces. "This place looks stocked."

"I'm ready to open. The sign will be going up out front tomorrow. 'Sinfully Sweet'." I placed the lid on his tub of treats. "Here you go."

"Thank you. That was really nice of you." He reached for the tub, our fingers touching.

I felt sparks where he touched me. That was new. It had never felt like that when David touched me.

"Th-that's okay." I smiled up at him. "I-I know how addictive they can be."

He placed the tub on the side next to us before he placed his hands on each side of me, caging me in. "Am I making you nervous?" he whispered. He reached up and pushed the hair back off the side of my neck.

"A little." I nodded my head. "You're looking at me like…"

"Like what?" he asked, interrupting. "Like I want you?" He dipped his head and inhaled against the column of my neck. "You smell good."

I gasped when I felt him press his body closer to mine. "I'm sorry, I…" I shook my head and placed my hands on his chest, pushing him back a little. "I'm not… After David, I don't think I'm ready for that. You're a great guy. It's just that—"

"It's just that he messed your head up," he finished for me.

"It's never easy catching your boyfriend cheating on you, Alex. I think it'd mess anyone's head up. I wouldn't want our friendship to be ruined by a one night stand."

He stared down at me for several moments before he stepped back.

"You wouldn't be a one night stand, darling." He picked the tub up and walked away, leaving me alone.

Stupid. Stupid. Stupid.

I reached behind me and untied my apron and hung it up behind the door. I quickly locked up the shop after turning everything off and made my way up the block to my apartment, cursing myself the whole way.

"What are you looking so happy about?" Addie asked sarcastically when I came through the door.

"I think I just upset Alex." I plonked myself down next to her on our sofa.

She frowned at me. "Upset how?"

"He tried to kiss me and I messed it up." I cringed as I looked at her.

"Charlie!" she whined. "He likes you and I know you like him. He's funny, runs his own business, is sexy as hell and wants you. What's the problem here?"

"David cheated on me, Adds. It was horrible walking in on them. What if the same thing happens again with Alex? I mean, look at him… If he cheated, I could lose the shop."

"Charlie…" She took my hand in hers and gave it a gentle squeeze. "If you keep measuring every guy up against what happened with David, you're always going to be the one who loses."

I stared at her for a moment. She seemed so open and honest.

"How do I fix it? How do I stop being so scared about messing this up? How do I get over him?"

"Sweetie." She wrapped her arm around my shoulders and pulled me into her side. "The only person holding you back is yourself. The first step is the hardest, but once you take it, you can be free. Free of him. Free of what he did to you."

I looked up at her.

"But first. You need to take that arse over to Alex's and take that first step." She tapped me comfortingly on my leg before she left me and headed to her bedroom.

Take that first step.

She made it sound so easy

Standing in front of my mirror, I turned to the side, checking my reflection. I frowned at the sight that reflected back at me. I was dressed in a loose, red top with a white bow on the collar and I had paired it with a pair of skinny jeans that were way too tight.

Shaking my head at myself, I was halfway to pulling my jeans down when Addie walked in.

"Leave them on!" she yelled while pointing her finger at me. "You look super-hot with them on and he won't be able to refuse you."

I rolled my eyes at her theatrics. "You sound like my pimp." I walked past her and took a seat on the sofa. After pulling my Ugg boots on, I did a little twirl. "How do I look?"

"If I was a lesbian, I'd go for you." She giggled before she tossed my jacket at me.

"Thanks." I slipped my denim jacket on and

grabbed my purse. After adding a coat of lipstick, I gave her a wave and left the building, making my way down the street to Alex's bar.

I came to a stop outside and took a sneaky look through the window. I was hoping he was working tonight. I would much rather do this in the bar than someplace more private. I didn't think I was ready to be alone with him just yet. I think we'd have to work up to that. I rolled my shoulders before walking inside.

He was standing at the bar, laughing at something that James was saying. It was hard to think of them as brothers as they didn't really look alike.

Alex looked over James's shoulder, the smile dropping from his face when he saw me.

"H-hi." I lifted my hand and lamely waved at him.

"Charlie." He walked up the bar a little, coming closer to where I was standing. "What can I do for you?"

"It's quiet tonight."

"Tomorrow it'll pick up. Thursday nights are for our curry people. The place will be busy." He winked at me. "It's a good job I have a decent cook," he said in a louder voice.

"Decent?" James laughed. "You're bloody lucky I went to cooking school." He gave me a salute and picked his plate up and walked to the kitchen.

"Take a seat," Alex said, waving his hand toward an empty stool. "What can I get for you?"

"I'll have a raspberry gin and lemonade, please." I took a seat and placed my purse on the bar-top. "Am I too late for food?"

I watched him turn and pour some gin into a glass and added some lemonade and ice to it. He popped a straw in and slid it across to me. "The kitchen is still open." He stared at me for a moment before speaking again. "I'm sorry about earlier," he apologised. "I shouldn't have pushed."

"You don't have to apologise." I shook my head. "I'm sorry. Earlier just surprised me is all."

"Surprised you how?" He leaned his elbows on the bar, resting his weight against it.

"When I was with David..." I looked at his chest, attempting to avoid his gaze. "I've only ever been with him and..." I sighed. "I just didn't expect to find someone so soon that would make me want that again."

He reached across and tilted my chin up. "Is it too fast?" he asked. His chocolate brown orbs stared into mine, stripping me bare.

"No." I shook my head. "Just unexpected."

"So, would it be unexpected if I asked to join you for dinner?" He smiled at me.

I shook my head. "No. That'd be really nice."

CHAPTER
Four

Alex

"So, what did you think?" James asked. He reached for our empty plates.

"It was very yummy," Charlotte replied. "Although pineapple is also very tasty on a pizza."

"What?" James looked insulted. "Pineapple does *not* belong on a pizza. That's vile."

She giggled at him before she looked at me. "What do you think, Alex?" she asked, putting me on the spot.

I laughed, shaking my head. "I think I'd have to agree with James. I've never tasted it, but fruit on a pizza?" I wrinkled my nose at her in distaste.

"Don't knock what you haven't tried." She wagged her finger at me in a teasing way and reached for her glass. "Can I have another?"

"Sure. Gin?" I reached for her glass but stopped when she shook her head.

"Can I have a coke instead?" She opened her purse. "How much do I owe you?"

"Nothing." I filled her glass with coke and ice and placed it in front of her. "It's on me."

She pulled a note out and reached over, stuffing it in the tip jar. She grinned at me wickedly. "Tonight has been fun," she admitted. "Maybe we can do this again some time?"

"Are you asking me out on a date, Miss Chase?" I teased. I loved the blush that appeared on her cheeks.

"I guess I am." She bit her bottom lip, looking sexy as fuck when she did that.

I reached across the bar for her hand, loving when she immediately offered hers to me. I gently grasped her fingers and brought her knuckles to my lips, kissing her soft skin. Before I could try for more than her hand, we were interrupted by the doors opening behind her.

"Well, well," a voice slurred. "What's going on here?" David leaned his drunken self against the wall and walked towards the bar. He wobbled over to us and took the stool a few seats down.

Charlotte sat with hunched shoulders, staring down at her drink.

I fucking hated it. The second that arsehole appeared, all her confidence just drained from her. Right now, she wasn't the sexy woman that had me tied up in knots. Instead, I was looking at David's victim. I knew it was more than a case of him cheating on her. I could imagine him putting her down and hurting her emotions.

"I can throw him out," I said quietly. I wouldn't lose anything by tossing him out on his arse.

"No." She shook her head forcefully. At the same time, she reached out and grabbed my arm. "Just serve him. It's not worth it."

I walked down the bar to him. "What can I get for you?"

He stared at me for a while before he curled his lip. He looked disgusted. "Are you fucking her?" he muttered quietly.

"Excuse me?" Was he for fucking real? He did *not* just fucking say that to me.

"I said," he yelled loudly, "are you fucking my girl?"

Charlie squeaked in surprise, staring at us. She looked mortified. She also looked scared.

"You had best lower your tone," I threatened. We were attracting the attention of several customers. "If you can't be civil, I'll be forced to throw you out." I was relieved when I saw James coming out of the kitchen and heading in our direction—not relieved because I couldn't throw this arsehole out on my own: more relieved because I was afraid that David may lash out at Charlie from their side of the bar.

"It didn't take you long to find someone else, did it?" he muttered at her.

"That's it. Get out." I walked around the bar and grabbed him by his arm, helping him off the chair and escorting him to the exit. I yanked the door open and tossed him through. "Stay out. You're barred."

James nodded his head at me and planted himself in the doorway. He would stay there for a while to keep him out.

I turned back to face Charlotte, hating the way that she had closed in on herself. Her shoulders were still hunched, and she was fiddling with the strap on her purse. "I'm so sorry, Alex," she whispered.

I walked over and placed myself in front of her. I reached down and tilted her chin up, forcing her eyes on me. "Stop apologising for that waste of space." I tilted my head in the direction of where I'd tossed him through the main doors. "If he ever bothers you again, I want you to tell me. Okay?"

She bit her lip and slowly nodded her head. "Okay," she whispered. "I'm still very sorry about..."

"Hush." I lifted my hand and pressed a finger against her lips. I felt them morph into a smile before I dropped my hand... "Now, where were we before we were so rudely interrupted?"

She giggled before responding. "I think I was asking you out on a date."

"You free tomorrow? I thought that we could go out

and toast your new venture." I was fucking loving the blush.

"I'd like that." She nodded her head. "I should be going home now." She slid off the barstool and grabbed her purse from where it was sitting on the bar-top.

"I'll walk you home. He should be gone by now but better safe than sorry." I walked her out the door, stopping by James. "I'm going to walk Charlotte home. Watch the bar until I get back."

He nodded at me and waved at Charlotte and walked back inside.

We fell into sync together and began the walk up the block to her apartment. I wasn't normally a paranoid person, but after tonight, my paranoia was knocked up a few levels. Since I'd seen David hanging outside her building, I hadn't thought anything of it. After tonight, though, I was confident that he could be a problem.

"You okay?" She looked up at me. "You're kind of freaking me out with the way that you're looking around."

I laughed. "It's nothing. I didn't mean to freak you out." I paused before changing the subject. "So, earlier you said that you had an early start tomorrow. What are you doing?"

The corners of her lips turned up before she spoke. "I am making some tasty desserts for my first customer. The sign fitters are also coming. I'm so excited to see it! 'Sinfully Sweet'. Do you like it?"

I loved the sparkle that she had in her eyes when she talked about her shop. "I love it." We came to a stop outside her building. "So, I'll see you tomorrow now, then."

"Okay. Come by and see me around three, and I will have your desserts boxed up and ready for you."

I reached down and tucked a loose curl behind her ear. "Maybe some caramel bites, as well?" I teased.

She giggled. I loved hearing that sound. She had a child's laugh and I wanted to hear it on repeat.

"I may have made some extras for you."

"You spoil me." I looked down at her lips before looking back up at her eyes. "I'm going to kiss you," I whispered.

She nodded her head and reached her hand out, sliding it up over my chest and resting her hand on my shoulder.

I took her face in my hands, dipping my head and pressed my lips to hers. I kept it soft and gentle, not wanting to push it too far. I pulled back before the temptation could get too much. I wanted to crush her to me and show her how much I wanted her.

"Go on inside. I'll see you tomorrow." I gave her a wink, attempting to keep things light.

She nodded and ducked her head and went through her main door, taking the stairs and disappearing from sight.

I turned around and walked back to the bar, eager for tomorrow.

Walking inside, I walked past the bar where James was standing. "All go okay?" I asked, referring to David.

"Yeah. I think you may have a problem there. I've seen him hanging around here a lot lately."

"You and me both." I looked around and saw that it was still pretty quiet. "Do you mind watching the bar for the rest of the night and locking up?"

He smirked at me. "Going somewhere?"

"Yes. A long, cold shower." I ignored the laughter that followed me.

"Dude. She is so out of your league," he called after me.

Don't I fucking know it.

The following day, I kept staring at the clock, watching the hands tick closer to three pm.

"You're like a fucking girl. Just go next door and get your cakes."

I rolled my eyes at James, doing what he said and leaving the bar. I gazed up, seeing that the sign for her shop had been fitted. I took a few steps back to check it out. It was written in cursive writing in a mix of pinks and yellows. It looked pretty good.

Walking inside, I headed to the back of the shop, stopping in the doorway.

Charlotte was standing at the square unit that was placed in the centre of the room. She had several dishes and boxes placed on there with her shop's logo printed on them. She seemed determined. She was going to make this place a success.

She turned around, jumping in surprise when she saw me. "You frightened me." She placed her hand on her chest before smiling.

"Sorry." I raised my hands in defeat and walked closer. "I'm early." I looked at her and saw a plate of covered caramel bites. "I've been thinking of those treats all day."

"I've made a monster out of you." She grinned at me and untied her apron, placing it on the side. "I've made a selection of caramel bites, gateaux, those mini desserts we talked about and I even made an apple tart with some custard for you."

"You're definitely spoiling me." I took a step closer to her. "You have sugar on you." I reached down and trailed my finger over her cheek before moving my fingers down her arm, taking her fingers in my palm. Little sparks ignited when our fingers linked.

She looked up at me before she shocked the hell out of me. She reached up on her toes and grabbed me by my top, pulling me down towards her. Our lips connected and I let myself pull her towards me. She parted her lips for me before I felt her tongue thrust in between my parted lips.

I spun us around and pressed her up against the worktop that ran around the edge of the room. I moved her arms up around my neck and reached down and placed my hand on her hips. I lifted her up and put her arse down on the surface. I stepped between her parted legs, loving the moan that came from her.

She tore her lips from mine, taking in a deep breath. Seconds later, she brought her mouth back to mine, kissing me passionately.

I grabbed her thighs, needing to feel her, but before I could make another move, we were disturbed by a voice from the doorway.

"Well, this is awkward."

I turned around and groaned when I saw a smirking Addie standing in the doorway. I stepped back when I felt Charlie pushing against my chest.

She scrambled down and pushed herself in front of me. "Uh, yes? What's up?"

"You said you'd need help carrying packages to the bar next door?" She cocked an eyebrow at us. "Do you need help with those packages now or...?"

I grinned at the way that she emphasised the word 'packages'. She made it sound dirty. I think that was a part of Addie's charm, though.

"Thank you." Charlie didn't sound too impressed.

"If you can grab those by there," she said, pointing to a few cake boxes, "and Alex and I will grab the rest."

"Sure." She grabbed the boxes and walked out the door, trying—and failing—to keep the smirk off her face.

Charlie chuckled when she left. "I'll pay for that one later."

I took her hand and pulled her back to me. "Don't worry about it. Come and hang out with me tonight."

"I thought we were going on a date to toast my new venture?" she asked.

"We could." I kissed her lips again and pulled back. "I'd rather it just be me and you, though." I looked down at her, trying to read her expression before she nodded.

"That'd be nice," she whispered. "Just me, you and most likely some caramel bites."

CHAPTER

Five

Charlie

Standing outside Alex's bar, I frowned when I saw David standing down the block. He looked like he was out with the boys. He lifted his head, catching me staring. I quickly ducked my head and slipped through the main doors. Running into my ex wasn't on tonight's agenda.

I gave a small wave to James standing at the bar.

"Go on back, Charlie." He nodded his head behind him. "Take the stairs up."

I nodded before following his directions. Taking the stairs, I placed my hand on the wooden barrier, trying to steady my nerves.

"There she is." Alex appeared in his doorway and held his hand out to me. "You okay?"

"Nervous." I let out a light chuckle.

"Come on in." His fingers tightened around mine as he pulled me into his apartment. "I made us some toasted paninis. A little birdy told me that you love cheese and ham."

"Should we call her Addie?" I giggled at him. "Thank you." He held the chair out for me.

"Would you like some wine?" He looked down at me.

"I'll have whatever you're having."

He grabbed a couple of bottles of Bud from the fridge. "This okay?" He held the bottles out, waiting for me to agree.

I nodded before slipping my cardigan off and hung it on the back of the chair. "So, how does a date with Alexander Winters normally go? Do you wine and dine all your girls?" I grinned at him, trying to show that I was teasing.

He laughed. "Wow, straight to the point." He rubbed his knuckles against the top of his head. "I don't usually date, to be honest. I usually just..."

"Oh." I was equal parts disappointed and relieved with his response: disappointed because I knew that he was a player who had undoubtedly been with many women, and relieved because I didn't like the idea of being jealous over the thought of some ex-girlfriends coming back for round two. "I see." I looked down at the table, not really sure what else to say after that.

He reached out and tilted my chin up to face him. "I've never dated anyone before." He leaned over and softly kissed my lips before pulling back.

"Then why am I here?" I asked. "If you don't normally date?"

"Because you," he said, blowing out a breath before continuing. "You have me tied up in knots and I find you sexy as hell." He grinned at me and stood up, grabbing our plates. He placed them down on the table. "And the idea of you with anyone else makes me crazy." He took a seat next to me and took a bite of his panini.

"I don't think anyone has ever said that to me before." I took a small bite, moaning at the taste. "That's so good."

We finished our paninis in silence before I spoke again. "You didn't tell me you could cook," I complimented. I wiped my lips with the napkin. "Just one of the many mysteries of Alex Winters, I guess."

"You think I'm mysterious?" He grinned. "Does it add to my charm?"

I frowned at him, looking down at the bangle on my wrist. "I don't..." I shook my head. "I don't like mysterious. My last relationship was mysterious. Mysterious usually involves secrets." I looked back up at him. "I don't date liars, Alex."

He frowned at me before he reached over. He took my face in his hand, resting his palm against my cheek and stroked his thumb over my cheekbone. "He hurt you, didn't he?" His beautiful brown eyes locked with mine. "Badly. More than you show the world, I mean."

"He cheated on me, Alex." I reached up and placed my hand over his wrist. "That hurt me more than I ever thought was possible."

"Did you love him?" he asked.

"I want to say yes, but I don't know." I shook my head. "When he did what he did... I wasn't broken. I moved on after a few weeks and got my life together. When I saw him cheating on me... You only get one chance with me, Alex. We all make mistakes, but if a guy cheats on me, that's it."

"That sounds like a warning." He leaned back. He wasn't smiling at me anymore.

"It's not a threat. I'd like to think that you wouldn't do that to me." I reached across the table, resting my hand on top of his.

He turned his hand and took my fingers in his before bringing them to his lips. "Come with me." He pulled me up by my hand and took me into the lounge and took a seat on the sofa. He gently pulled me down next to him and placed his arm around my shoulders, stroking his fingers over my upper arm.

"Are you okay?" I asked. "You look kind of tense."

"I want to tell you that I will never treat you like that arsehole did." He turned to me suddenly and took my face in both of his palms. "One chance with you.

That's all I want. One chance to make you my girl." He looked so open and honest. "To make you mine."

I wanted to trust him so badly, but I was afraid— afraid he would hurt me more than David ever did.

"Kiss me," I whispered. "Kiss me and show me what it means to be your girl."

As soon as the words had left my lips, he dipped his head and pressed his own to mine. I moaned at the contact. I parted my lips, slipping my tongue in between his parted ones. I reached up and took a hold of the collar of his t-shirt and turned my body towards his.

He wrapped his arm around the bottom of my back, tugging me closer to him until we were facing each other. He reached down and lifted my legs, placing them over his.

"This okay?" he asked.

I nodded before tugging him back to me. "I like kissing you."

He chuckled against my lips before kissing me back. His kisses were nice: soft and sweet but also rough and passionate. He trailed his hand up my leg, not stopping until he was palming my upper thigh.

I tore my lips from his, reaching down and stopping his movements. "Too fast," I gasped.

"I'm sorry." He looked down at me and tucked a loose curl back behind my ear. "I, uh..." He cleared his throat. "I wouldn't expect sex on the first date."

I widened my eyes at him in surprise. "Wow. That was blunt."

"I didn't mean that I asked you here to have sex." He chuckled. "Wow, I am great at putting my foot in my mouth tonight, aren't I?"

I giggled at the look of mortification on his face. "I think it's one of your skills." I reached over and dug him in the ribs. "I get what you're trying to say. Sex is usually a part of your dating routine. Or, *not* dating routine, I guess."

"Sex usually happens when I'm with someone, yeah." He rubbed his palm over my leg. "I know it's too early for you and..." He sighed. "I can wait. Dating is new for me, so I think getting to know each other better first might be—"

"Thank you," I said, interrupting him. I was touched by what he said.

"You're welcome." He leaned down and kissed me again. "Just don't keep me waiting too long." He gave me a cheeky wink as he wrapped his arm around me, pulling me into his side. "How about we watch a movie?"

"I'd like that." I smiled up at him, cuddling closer into his side, feeling comfortable in his arms.

"*S*o, how did the date go?" Addie asked. She took a bite from her chocolate donut. "Did you guys...?" She wiggled her eyebrows at me.

"No!" I denied. "No. Geez, Adds. It's a bit soon for sex, don't you think?"

"Well, it's not like you guys are strangers." She shrugged her shoulders. "I mean, you guys have known each other for a while. It's not like..."

"But we are," I disagreed. "Strangers, I mean. Any time before this, whenever we saw each other, I was either with David or you. It's not like we ever actually knew each other besides the odd civil conversation to be polite."

"I guess I didn't think of it like that. You like him though, don't you? I mean, it's not like you're afraid, right?"

"I'm afraid, a little," I admitted. "David was... a challenge. He was—could be—difficult."

"You can say that again." She pointed her finger at me. "Alex is a good guy, though. I don't think he'd ever treat you like that moron did."

"We had the whole cheating conversation last night," I admitted. I focused on the pot of sauce I was stirring. "He said that..."

"No, sweetie." She got off her stool and came around the worktop. Taking me by the shoulders, she turned me to face her, halting my stirring activity.

"David treated you terribly. He never complimented you, always acted like you were his property and he..." She frowned at me and I hated the sympathy that I could see reflected in her eyes. "He never appreciated you, Charlie." She reached her arms out and pulled me into a hug. "Alex knows I'd kick his arse and pluck his eyebrows out if I ever caught him doing that to you."

We both laughed.

"I had better get going so that I can have a bath before tonight's shift." She pulled back, picking her donut back up and walking towards the door.

"Hold up," I said. "I want to talk to you about your job."

She turned to me, looking confused. "What about my job?"

"How would you like to work here?" I held my arms out, indicating our surroundings. "Not to cook," I rushed to explain. "I was thinking, you could be more of a waitress and help out on the counters. I think— well, I'm hoping—that I'll be kept busy in the kitchen through the day, and I would rather have you here than some random stranger."

"Really? You'd want me here with you?" She looked so doubtful.

"Of course!" I grabbed her hands and entwined our fingers. "You're my best friend. Us working together would be amazing. Please tell me you'll think about it."

"I'll do more than think about it. I'll hand my

resignation in this evening." She wrapped her arms around me and hugged me, squeezing me extra tightly before letting me go. "Thank you, Charlie," she whispered.

I let her go, watching her walk out of the door. I hated thinking of where she would be tonight. My best friend was beautiful—inside and out—and she deserved better than being stuck dancing around some pole.

I turned around when I heard the door opening behind me and smiled when I saw Alex standing there, holding a bunch of beautiful, long-stemmed daisies.

"Are they for me?" I was so touched. "No one has ever bought flowers for me before."

"Really?" He frowned at me and walked closer to me. "Never? He never once bought you...?" He shook his head at me before he dipped his head and kissed my cheek.

"They are beautiful." I took the stems from him and inhaled the scent. "Daisies are my favourite flower."

"I know." He grinned at me. "Here." He took the flowers from me. "Let me put those in some water for you." He picked the glass vase up off the sill and filled it with some water, cutting the ends of the stems off and placing them in the water.

"You're looking very domesticated over there, Alex." I couldn't stop myself from teasing him.

"I'll show you domesticated," he threatened. Before I could try to escape, his arm wrapped around my waist and pulled me into him, with my back to his chest. He moved down and pressed his lips to my neck.

"I'd love to see you try and domesticate me." He chuckled against my skin, his warm breath tickling me. "Can I see you this weekend?" He placed his hands on my hips and turned me around slowly to face him.

"I can't this weekend." I slid my hands up over his shoulders. "I need to focus on getting everything ready for the grand opening on Monday. Is that okay?"

"Of course. It's going to be amazing." He dipped his head and pecked my lips before moving back. "I'll be here to celebrate with you on Monday." He winked at me before pulling back and leaving me.

CHAPTER
Six

Alex

The day had finally arrived. 'Sinfully Sweet' opened this morning and the place looked really busy.

"How's it going?" I asked, stopping at the ice cream counter where Addie had a queue of kids.

"She's in the kitchen. Don't I look great in my uniform?" She stuck her chest out to indicate where her name was written on her left breast. The logo was on the middle of her pink top.

I laughed at the way the teenage boy next to me looked at her. His eyes widened in shock and I knew that Addie would most likely be featuring in his one-handed fantasy tonight.

I walked away, leaving her to it and made my way

back to the kitchen. I gave a small wave to the other member of staff that was at the till. I didn't recognise her but she seemed friendly enough.

"There you are!" I grinned at the sight of her. She had flour all over her 'Sinfully Sweet' t-shirt and had trays of donuts laid out on the counters in front of her. "They are for me, yes?" I went to reach for one but stopped when she smacked my hand away.

"Not so fast, mister." She came around the worktop and hugged me, wrapping her arm up around my neck. "You can get your sugar here." She giggled at my look of surprise before she leaned up on her toes and kissed me, sucking my lip in between hers.

"I'm liking this." I tilted my head, pressing my lips harder against hers.

"I can't do that here," she whispered, pulling back. "I'm sorry."

"Don't be sorry." I stepped back. "You're busy. I shouldn't have come by, but I wanted to check and see how you were doing."

"It's crazy! I only expected a few customers and it hasn't stopped." She went to the fridge and pulled out some tubs of chocolate mouse and yellow custard. "Can I see you later?" she asked.

"I'd like that." I leaned back over and kissed her sweet lips again. "I'm off work tonight, so just come on up to my apartment. I'll leave the door open for you."

"Okay. Bye." She gave me a small wave before she

began adding sprinkles and chocolate curls to the donuts.

I walked back through the café area of the shop, giving a two-fingered salute to Addie and disappearing back next door.

"How's our girl doing?" James asked.

I glared at him, not liking how comfortable he was at calling her 'our girl'.

He laughed at me before holding his hand up in defeat. "We can call her your girl. Whatever."

"I'll be upstairs," I replied. I didn't like how fucking jealous I was at the idea of someone else laying claim to her, least of all my own brother. "Scott will be by later to help you out with the bar. Any problems, give me a shout."

"I'll send her up, shall I?" he called after me.

Fucker was a wind-up.

Sitting at the table in my kitchen, I spent most of the afternoon catching up on paperwork: taxes, stock take, supplier checks... The hours quickly vanished, and before I knew it, evening had descended.

I was disturbed from the figures in front of me when a pair of hands covered my eyes.

"Guess who," a sexy voice sang in my ear.

I reached behind me and pulled Charlie into my lap, sitting her across me so that her legs were dangling to one side. "How was your first day, beautiful?" I wrapped my arms around her waist, anchoring her to me.

"Hectic," she groaned. She laced her arms around my neck. "But so much fun!"

"I'm proud of you." I rubbed my thumbs against the skin on her hip. "You did amazing today."

"Thank you." That beautiful pink blush once again stained her cheeks. "I'm pretty proud of me, too." She dipped her head, kissing me, before straightening back up.

"Do you want some dinner?" I asked. "We have some..."

"No." She shook her head. "I just want to be here with you."

With me? Did she mean....?

"Are you sure?" I tilted my head back, looking up at her. "You don't have to feel pressured to be with me in that way."

"I know." She shrugged her shoulders. "I haven't been with a man in over a year, Alex."

David was a fucking fool. He had a sexy as sin woman, completely devoted to him, and instead, he was out screwing every other woman that he could get his hands on. The man had to be fucking crazy.

"Why so long?" I asked. I needed to know why. I needed to know why the fuck she'd put up with his bullshit for so long. "Why did you put up with it?" I asked. "Why didn't you see that you deserved better?"

"I trusted him," she whispered. "I didn't want to admit that we were wrong. That what we *had* was wrong." She slid her hands up, trailing her fingers up the column of my neck. "Being here with you, like this..." She dipped her head and kissed behind my ear. "This feels right."

When I felt her chest pressed against mine, I snapped. I fisted my hand in the back of her hair and pulled her lips forcefully down to mine and thrust my tongue in between them. She moaned at my action before she crushed her upper body against mine more. Before she could move again, I stood us up and placed her arse down on my table.

"If you want me to stop, you had better say something now." I looked down at her swollen lips and rubbed my thumb across them.

"And if I don't?" she asked. It felt like she was taunting me.

"If you don't," I replied. "I'm going to take you into my bedroom and you won't be leaving it till morning."

She tilted her head back and stared into my eyes for a few moments before she lifted her hand and thread it through my hair. "Why did you never tell me?" she asked.

"Why did I never tell you what?" I asked, the question confusing me.

"Why did you never tell me that you wanted me?" She nibbled her bottom lip. "I see the way you watch me." Her words were confident but the blush on her cheeks had turned to a darker pink, giving away how embarrassed she was. "I'd always thought that we were just friends."

"We were," I quickly defended. "I was always your friend, but you were his. You belonged to him." I chuckled. "I may be an arsehole, but I don't go hitting on other men's girls."

"I'm not his now," she whispered. She leaned forward and kissed me, sucking on my bottom lip. "Didn't you mention something about taking me into your bedroom?" She giggled before kissing me again.

I groaned against her lips before reaching down and grasping her legs. "Wrap them around me," I whispered against her lips.

"Don't drop me." She placed her arms around my neck, holding her upper body closer to mine. The action brought her chest to my eye level, and she was making it harder for me to control my wicked thoughts. She had no fucking idea how much I wanted her. She had no idea how tightly wound she had me.

I kicked the bedroom door shut behind me and gently placed her down on the bed. I kneeled back to give her a little space, not wanting her to feel pressured.

She reached down and grasped the hem of her t-shirt and began pulling it up.

"Stop." I halted her, placing my hand on her wrist to stop her actions. "We don't have to do this."

"Don't you want to?" she asked. "I mean…"

"I do." I looked down at her, loving how right she was lying there. "I have wanted you for long enough." I rubbed the outside of her thigh, trying to be comforting. "I can wait if you are not ready."

"I'm ready." She fisted the front of my t-shirt and pulled me down to her. "I think we have waited long enough, don't you?" She kissed me, pouring passion into it. She parted her legs more so that I could fit in between them. Her hands slid beneath the bottom of my t-shirt before she scraped her nails against my skin.

I pulled back, needing her to know something before this escalated further. "I'm not soft or gentle, darling." I placed my hands on either side of her head, leaning my weight on them. "I'd never hurt you but I…"

"I don't want soft or gentle, Alex." She reached up and placed her hands on my shoulders. "I've had soft and gentle." She grinned up at me, obviously reading in my eyes how much the thought of her having had soft and gentle with someone else made me feel. "I just want you."

Fuck, I was so screwed with her.

"Alex, stop thinking so much." She looked up at me and I could see no fear or worry reflecting back at me. "Just be here with me. Just you and me. Together."

I nodded and let her pull me down to her lips. I reached down and slid my hands beneath her t-shirt, spanning the width of her stomach with my hands.

She pushed me to the side and climbed on top of me. She reached down and grabbed the bottom of her top and slowly began pulling it up her body. She tossed it to the side before she began pushing my t-shirt up my chest. I reached behind me and grabbed the back of it and yanked it up and over my head, tossing it aside and pulled her back down to me.

"You look so fucking beautiful." I reached up and palmed her bra-covered breast, gently squeezing it.

She moaned at my touch before I felt her rotate her hips against me, causing friction. "That feels good," she whispered. She dipped her head, seeking out my lips.

I fisted the back of her hair, forcing her down against me. I reached down and grasped her arse, but before we could get any further, we were interrupted by my bedroom door slamming open against the wall.

"Dude! What the fuck?" I snapped at James standing in the open doorway.

I moved Charlie aside and covered her with the blanket, not appreciating the way that his eyes were lingering on her.

"Outside!" I nodded my head towards the lounge before grabbing my t-shirt and forcing him back out the way he came in. I shut the door behind me, restraining myself from slamming it closed the way that I wanted to. "What do you want?" I asked.

"We have a problem downstairs." His eyes shot behind me when Charlie came through the door.

"Problem how?" I crossed my arms, still not appreciating being interrupted.

He looked behind me at Charlie coming out of my bedroom.

"Is everything okay?" she asked. She reached down and took my hand in hers, entwining our fingers.

"You need to come downstairs," he said and turned around and walked out of the apartment.

I sighed, following him through the door and down the stairs. I kept my grasp on Charlie's hand before coming to a stop beside the bar-top. There was smashed glass all over the floor and the window at the centre of the front of the storefront was put through. There was a large brick on the floor amongst wood splinters from a turned over table. Large shards of glass were still attached to the frame. I looked over to the right and saw several customers were huddled away from the damage. They seemed scared and very concerned.

"What happened?" I ground out.

"Everything was normal," James replied, turning around to face us. "I was serving that family of four over there when suddenly there was a loud screeching noise of brakes and then that brick came flying through the window. Luckily, it didn't hit any customers, but it could have done some serious damage."

"This is awful." Charlie gasped at my side. "Who do you think did it?"

I looked at James, knowing full well who fucking did

it. He subtly nodded his head at me before he walked past me. "I'll go and get a dustpan and brush to clean this mess up."

"I'll go and help him," Charlie said, following him back to the storeroom.

After apologising to the customers and offering some complimentary freebies for their next visit, I watched them leave before locking up. I quickly took some photographs of the damage for insurance purposes and then took a seat at one of the booths.

That fucking ex of hers was going to regret taking me on.

CHAPTER

Seven

Charlie

Sitting on a barstool watching James brush the debris away, I was filled with guilt and remorse. Neither of them would say it, but we all knew who had done this. It didn't take a rocket scientist to figure it out.

"Go on up," he said, breaking the silence. "He needs someone tonight."

Alex had silently disappeared up to his apartment a half-hour ago. His shoulders had been slumped and he'd looked like he had the weight of the world on his shoulders.

"He's so upset," I whispered. "This is all because of me." I was so ashamed. I had now dragged Alex and

James and their respectable business into my stupid break-up. "He probably hates me now."

"Go on up," James said, repeating his words. "He'll talk to you."

I nodded before taking the stairs slowly, feeling dread settle in my stomach. I wouldn't have been surprised if he threw me out and asked to never see me again. I grasped the door handle and slowly opened the door, stepping inside. The lounge was empty and so was the kitchen so that left only the bedroom. I knocked gently on the door and walked in.

"I'm sorry," I whispered.

Alex was sitting on the end of his bed looking completely depressed. He gazed up at me before he raised his hand to me. "Come here, darling." He waved me closer until he could grasp my hand to pull me down into his lap. "I'm sorry. I just needed a moment to think."

"I'm the one that's sorry, Alex." I linked my arms around his neck. "It's my fault this happened."

"What makes you say that?" He stared up at me and I hated the fake look of innocence that was pasted on his face.

"I think this may be too much too fast."

He frowned at me, not even bothering to mask the look of hurt on his face.

"David was in here shouting about us the other day and now this…" I shook my head. "I just think we should maybe calm down things a little." I planned to stand up and leave him while I go home and pretend that my words weren't affecting me, but instead, his arms tightened around me.

"Don't go," he whispered. "I'm not letting you go."

"Are you going to chain me to your bed?" I asked sarcastically. The giggle died in my throat when I saw the look of lust appear on his face. His eyes dipped down to my lips before I felt his hardness grow beneath me.

"Stay with me tonight," he whispered.

"I shouldn't..." I felt his arms loosen from around me and I stood, leaving his embrace. "I think we should take what happened tonight as a sign and just..."

"I don't care about what happened tonight." He reached up and took my face in his hands. "Stay with me tonight and when tomorrow comes, we can deal with it then."

I looked down at him, trying to get the strength to continue with my plan, but as I stared at him, I realised that I didn't want to walk away from him. I liked the way that he didn't want to let me go.

"No sex," he promised. "I will try and be a gentleman."

I giggled before nodding my head, giving in to him. "I hope you don't have cold feet."

I let him lead me to the side of the bed and kicked off my shoes before climbing in. I scooted over until I was in the middle and waited for him to turn off the light and join me.

He slid his arm around my waist and pulled my back against his chest.

"Good night, Alex," I whispered.

He dipped his head and kissed my cheek. "Good night, darling."

———

I was somewhere between sleep and awake when I felt movement. Soft, gentle fingers began stroking their way up and down my arm, stirring me from dreamland. Little sparks bloomed out from his touch.

"Time to wake up, sweetheart," Alex whispered before he kissed my cheek.

"It's too early," I groaned. I turned my face into the pillow, attempting to hide my eyes from the rays of sunlight that were coming in through the window. "What time is it?" I asked.

"It's just past five am." He wrapped his arm around my waist, cuddling me closer. "You need to get up if you have to bake sugary treats for opening."

I groaned, knowing how right he was. If I didn't get into that kitchen in the next hour, I would be so screwed come opening time.

"I suppose"—he whispered, his fingers trailing

down to my stomach to stroke random patterns against my skin—"I could come up with a way to wake you up." He moved his palm further down and slipped his fingers beneath the waistband of my leggings. He stopped his movements and lowered his head, pressing his lips to my neck. "Is this okay?"

I nodded my head, tilting my head to the side, wanting his lips back on my skin. I placed my hand on his and guided his hand down lower. "Touch me," I whispered. I reached behind me and thread my fingers into the back of his hair.

He slipped his hand down further until his fingers were against my clit. He rubbed me before he kissed me softly, thrusting his tongue into my mouth.

I moaned against his lips, parting my legs more. "That feels good."

He slipped a finger inside of me before adding another. He thrust them, making me moan once again.

I sucked his tongue into my mouth and rocked my hips against his hand.

His wrist sped up, pulling moans of pleasure from me. The only sounds in the room were his fingers moving inside me and my moans being swallowed by his mouth.

"Come for me, my darling girl." He leaned down and sunk his teeth into my naked shoulder.

I tightened my grip in his hair as I came apart for him, calling out his name. I lay there a quivering mess, smiling when I felt his arms wind tighter around me.

"You're so fucking sexy when you're mid-orgasm."

I giggled at him. "I'm going to take that as a compliment."

"You definitely should." He leaned down and began kissing my neck, his tongue tasting my skin.

"Don't start that now," I groaned. "I need to get home and take a shower." I crawled out of bed, thankful he didn't try and keep me there. I had a feeling that if he tried to, it wouldn't take much effort on my part to let him.

He walked me downstairs through the bar, unlocking the door for me to go through. "Hold up," he said. He took my wrist and pulled me back to him. "Not so fast." He grinned down at me before lowering his head and kissing me. "Can I see you later?"

"Uh, I'm not sure."

His face dropped.

"I might have a girly night with Addie."

"Ah, I see." He had a bit of a cocky tone to his voice. "Girl time and maybe talk about the new guys in your life."

"You got it." I grinned and walked down the block, leaving him.

I was halfway down the block when I turned around, giggling when I saw he was still standing on the door. I gave him a wave and disappeared inside. After entering the apartment, I made my way straight to Addie's bedroom. She was awake but not out of bed yet.

"Are you only just getting up?" she asked. She reached up to wipe her eyes before sitting against the headboard. She looked down at my outfit before her eyes shot back up to mine. A look of shock appeared on her face. "You dirty slut! Did you spend the night at Alex's?" We both giggled at her insult. "Get over here and tell me everything!" She patted the side of her bed enthusiastically.

"I can't. I need to take a shower," I said, pointing my thumb over my shoulder in the direction of the bathroom door. "I have to get over to the shop and start baking."

"Fine." She had a mock-pout on her face. "You have to give me all the juicy details later though," she reasoned.

"Tonight?" I asked. "I was thinking we could have a girly night. Just me and you."

"Definitely." She nodded her head and lay back down. "I'm going to have another hour."

"That's fine. Just be there by nine am." I gave her a small wave and went back to my room.

I quickly stripped out of my clothes and grabbed my towel and headed to the bathroom. I closed the door and turned the shower on before stepping inside.

The water was hot and was already relaxing my stiff shoulders.

After soaping some shampoo into my hair, my thoughts drifted back to last night with Alex. It had been perfect. *He'd* made it perfect.

I spun around, frowning when I saw the bathroom door was wide open. I'd definitely closed that door. I turned back to the shower and washed the soap out of my hair and off my body before turning the faucet off and wrapping a towel around myself. I slowly walked to the doorway, hating how unnerved I was feeling. It wouldn't have been Addie: she wasn't a morning person and would certainly have fallen back asleep after I'd left her room.

I stepped through the doorway cautiously, not liking the path of goose bumps that had travelled up my arms. I froze in the lounge when I saw the door to my apartment wide open. I went to the door and quickly shut it before sliding the chain lock on and turning around to run straight to Addie's room. She was flat out, cuddling into her pillow, imitating a starfish.

I quickly checked my room, the lounge and kitchen and went back to my room. After drying off, I changed into a pair of jeans and a café branded t-shirt, adding a bit of foundation and mascara. I grabbed my keys and locked the apartment up, heading up the block to the shop.

The whole way there, I was looking over my

shoulders on the constant lookout for David. I hated to think that he could have broken into my apartment this morning but after last night, seeing the damage caused to Alex's place of work, I was at a loss as to who else it could be.

Who else would want to hurt us both? He was the only person I could think of.

After mixing up a batch of cookie dough, I set it out in uneven blobs on several baking trays and popped them in the oven. I looked around and after checking the counters, I was relieved to see that the only products I needed to stock up on were cupcakes, donuts, cookies and some caramel bites. They seemed very popular with the customers—not excluding Alex.

I reached for my phone and dialled Alex. I didn't like to take my dramas to him, but after last night, I know he'd hate to be left out of the loop.

"Missing me already?" he asked.

"I need to see you. I'm at the kitchen but I—"

"In the shop?" he asked.

"Yes. Right next door."

"On my way." He hung up on me. Several moments later, he came through the back door, not stopping until he was standing in between my parted legs. "What is it?"

"It's silly," I whispered, "but I thought you should know." I reached up and placed my hands on his wrists where he was holding my face in his hands. "I was taking a shower this morning and I…" I blew out a breath. "I was washing my hair when I heard the creak of a door. I turned around and my bathroom door was open."

He frowned at me and I could see the thoughts written on his face.

"I closed it, Alex. I know I closed it."

"It frightened you," he whispered. "Do you think maybe…?"

"That didn't frighten me." I shook my head at him before continuing. "My apartment door was wide open when I came out of the bathroom. *That's* what frightened me."

His jaw tensed and I knew that he was now worried.

"Do you believe me?" I asked.

"I do." He rubbed his hands up and down the outside of my thighs, comforting me with his touch. "Thank you for telling me."

"What do we do?" I asked.

"When you and Addie are at home, I want you to keep the lock chain on until I can come over and change the locks. Okay? We can do it this weekend."

I nodded my head before pulling him into a hug. "Thank you, Alex."

He turned his head and kissed my cheek. "Anytime, darling."

CHAPTER
Eight

Charlie

Walking home, I was exhausted. Today had been crazier than yesterday. I needed to start looking at suppliers for some products because if it continued like this, I'd have to start working through the night as well.

I had planned to go and see Alex to make sure he was okay after we'd chatted about my intruder, but come six pm, the only thing that I wanted was my bed, which wasn't going to happen considering I had promised girl time to Addie.

I slid the key into the lock and walked inside, turning and putting the chain across. I laughed when I saw the pile of DVD's stacked on the coffee table.

"You're finally home!" Addie came dancing out of

the kitchen wearing her red strappy vest and matching shorts. "I was starting to think that you had dumped me for your new guy." She wiggled her eyebrows at me.

"I thought about it." I giggled at her before dumping my bag on the worktop. "Let me go and get changed and then girl time needs to start." I turned around and headed to my bedroom. "Pour me a vodka, please," I called over my shoulder.

I quickly changed into my blue strappy top and pyjama trousers and walked back to the kitchen to join Addie. Before I could grab the Doritos and join her in the lounge, my phone rang from where it was inside my bag. I smiled when I saw it was Alex.

"Hi. Is everything okay?" I asked.

"Hey, darling. Of course, it is. I just wanted to check and see if I could change your lock earlier. Say Friday?"

"You sound worried." I didn't like to tease him because I knew he was freaked out over someone being able to just walk in here—more specifically David.

"Addie has a date on Friday night so we could do it after work?"

"I'll be there."

"Maybe you could stay the night if you don't have to be at the bar?" I asked nervously. "Maybe we could have some alone time just me and you?" I don't know why I ended it as a question.

"I'd like that. Have a good time later and I will see you on Friday."

"Bye, Alex," I said quietly.

"Bye, darling."

I hung up and walked into the lounge, chuckling when I saw that Addie already had the Dirty Dancing DVD playing. It was at the part where Baby was carrying a watermelon and her life was about to go upside down.

I took a seat next to her before tucking my legs beneath me. "So what're the plans for tonight?"

She handed me a vodka mixed with cranberry juice before leaning back against the cushion. "Tell me everything."

"Tell you what?" I asked.

She laughed. "Please. You start dating the hot bartender and you expect me not to ask?" She shook her head disappointedly. "First, I want to know what happened today. You've been in your own little world for most of today. What happened?"

I stared at Baby and Johnny on the screen. I was unsure of how to answer this question. "I took a shower this morning."

"Okay?" She was confused about why I was explaining my personal hygiene routine to her.

"I think someone was in the apartment. I felt someone watching me and when I came out of the bathroom, the door to the apartment was wide open."

Her eyes shot over my shoulder. "Is that why you've put the chain across tonight?"

I nodded. "I checked to see if anything was missing but I don't think there was. I checked on you and you were asleep."

"Do you think it was David?" she asked.

"Yes. I was at Alex's last night and someone put a window through in the bar. They think it was David."

"Why do they think that?" she asked. She looked shocked.

"He was in there a few evenings ago, yelling. Asking what was going on between me and Alex." I cringed, waiting for the influx of questions that I knew were coming.

"Why didn't you tell me?!" She smacked me lightly on my arm. "So David has gone crazy on us then." She sighed, raising her eyebrows. "I thought he was having trouble letting go but I didn't see this coming…"

"You did?" I asked. Now I was confused.

"I've seen him hanging around a few times." She shrugged her shoulders. "So have you." She leaned back and tapped her lap, gesturing for me to put my feet there.

"I know." I stretched my legs out, groaning when she began digging her thumbs into the arch of my foot. "He's the one that cheated, though. He's the one that ended this. Not me."

"I know." She nodded her head. "I think he thought you'd never walk. I think he thought that you would just take it—that you'd go back to him." She turned her head to face me. "You're better than that. You *deserve* better than that."

"Thanks, Addie." I smiled at her, loving how loyal she was. I'd expected her to get angry and start shouting at me for dragging her into my drama. "Alex is going to come over Friday evening and change our locks. He asked if we can keep using the chain lock when either of us are home until then."

"Not a problem." She stroked her finger up the centre of my foot, tickling the skin there. "Now, spill on the real gossip."

"What do you want to know?" I sighed resignedly before gulping down the rest of my drink. I took her glass off her and went to the kitchen, refilling our drinks and re-joining her back on the sofa.

"Tell me everything." She grinned at me before taking a sip. "Have you and he…?"

"No!" I defended. "No. But he might be here Saturday morning for breakfast."

"Message received." She clinked her glass against mine.

"What about you and James?" I asked, turning the questions back on her. "He's a good looking man."

"He is." She shook her head, crinkling her nose. "A lady never tells. Plus, I need a little bit of kink in my man, anyway."

"A little?" I mocked.

She giggled. "Okay. A lot." She tossed her head

back letting out a proper laugh. "I've missed our chats, Charlie. We used to do this more often."

"I know. I'm sorry. My head has been so full lately and I—"

"Uh, hello. You've just opened your own café and it's going amazingly!" She reached over and took my hand in hers before giving it a gentle squeeze. "I'm so proud of you."

"Thanks, Addie. I can't believe it's finally happening. I have to pinch myself sometimes…"

"Let's toast it." She held her glass up. "To 'Sinfully Sweet'."

"To friends." I smiled, holding my glass.

"To family," she whispered.

We clinked glasses before she placed her glass down on the coffee table and held her arms out for a hug.

I copied her actions, putting my glass down and shuffled closer to her and wrapped my arms around her.

"I'm so proud of you, Charlie." She turned her head and kissed my cheek. "So fucking proud."

"Thank you, Addie." I squeezed her extra tight before pulling away, leaning back and watching the rest of Dirty Dancing.

As the credits rolled, I cringed when a yawn escaped. "I'm sorry." I laughed. "I didn't realise how tiring this job was going to be."

"You can go to bed?" She ended it as a question.

"I'm going to hang out here and make a sexy Skype call later."

I laughed and leaned across, kissing her cheek. "So, if I hear any screams, I shouldn't be alarmed, then? See you in the morning." I gulped the rest of my drink down before dropping the glass off in the sink in the kitchen and disappearing to my room. After turning the light off, I climbed into bed. My phone lit up the dark room, alerting me to a text message.

I grabbed my phone, smiling when I saw who it was from.

Hope you had a good night with Addie. – A x

I smiled, secretly loving that his thoughts were obviously on me enough for him to send a text message.

It was lovely thanks. I just crawled into bed. – C x

I looked at the screen, smiling when I saw the bubble appear, telling me that he was typing something. After waiting for a few moments, I frowned when it disappeared. Seconds later, my phone rang with his name appearing on the screen.

I quickly answered it, still wondering why he hadn't replied to my message.

"You're a tease," he said before I could even say 'hello'.

"I am?"

"You know you are." I heard him sigh. "I'm stuck behind this bar imagining you in bed."

"Mr. Winters. You're making me blush." I giggled down the phone. I loved that he was comfortable enough to talk to me about this rather than a text message. "I thought you were a gentleman."

"I don't know what made you think that, darling."

Fuck, he had a sexy voice.

"I've got to go." He sighed down the phone. "Are we still on for Friday? I was thinking we could do Chinese or something."

"That sounds perfect. I'll see you on Friday."

"Sweet dreams, darling."

"Good night, Alex." I placed my phone on the cabinet beside my bed before turning over, snuggling my head into the pillow. I couldn't wipe the smile off my face, hoping it would follow me into my dreams.

Waking up the next morning, I groaned when I realised it was time to start the day. Looking at the clock, I saw that it was already ten minutes to six am, which meant I was already nearly half an hour late. I rolled to the side and swung my legs out of bed. Sitting on the side, my eyes still droopy, I knew that today was going to be a struggle. I stared at my reflection in the mirror, wondering if I could get away with passing on the shower until the evening.

One look in the mirror had me shaking my head: I looked like I had shaken Fester Addams' hand with the way that my hair was sticking up. It looked like a frizz-bomb had gone off.

I headed for the bathroom, hanging my towel on the rail by the shower door before shutting the door, and stripped out of my pyjamas. Climbing in, I stood, waiting for the water to warm up, standing beneath the faucet.

After washing some strawberry-scented shampoo into my hair, I used the pink, fuzzy loofah to soap up my body. As I washed my legs, I realised that I would have to shave them and other areas before Friday came.

Friday had to be nothing other than perfect.

CHAPTER
Nine

Alex

Sitting in the corner of the bar on Thursday night going over the financial figures from the last month's takings, I took a swig from the glass coke bottle on my table. Looking at the profit figures, it was clear that Thursday's curry evenings were our most popular nights. Each evening had a theme for our meals and the curries ensured the bar was always busy from six pm to ten-thirty.

I always made sure to keep the 'normal' dishes running alongside the themed dishes so that I still attracted the customers who weren't keen—like me—on being forced to eat a particular type of cuisine.

I looked across at a table of four—two kids and their parents—smiling when I saw their little girl eating her slice of chocolate cake. She had chocolate all over her mouth and she appeared like she was loving it.

"Looks like Charlie's desserts are going down well." James placed a burger and fries down in front of me with a tub of tomato sauce.

"I knew they would." I ticked a few numbers off before dunking a fry in the sauce. "Any more trouble since the whole window incident?" I waved my hand towards the now-repaired window.

"Nothing." He shook his head. "I had a word with the boys—Scott and John included—and I have told them to report any funny business to either you or me."

"Good plan." I nodded my head at the stool opposite me. "I need you to cover me Friday night. I have a date with Charlie."

"How is the shop going?" he asked while stealing a fry. "I see the people going up and down. Seems pretty popular."

"She's doing really well." I could feel the smile forming on my face. "I knew she'd do well."

"So, uh…" He coughed to clear his throat. "What are you going to do about her ex? I didn't realise how much of a loose screw he was." He didn't give me a chance to answer before he was on to the next question. "Does Addie know about him strolling into their apartment?"

"If it *was* him," I reason. "There's no evidence that

it was actually him. Just because he put my window through…"

"Bullshit! You don't believe that." He had his eyebrows raised in surprise at me.

"No, I don't." I tossed my pen down on the ledger. "It makes me feel better to deny it, though."

"Just watch your back." He pointed his thumb to the bar before he grabbed another fry and walked back to the kitchen.

I gazed over at Scott and saw that David was sitting on a barstool. He was continuously looking around the bar. He couldn't see me sitting in the corner. It was one of the reasons why I sat here: peace and fucking quiet was hard to get in this place.

After devouring my burger and fries, I waved at Scott to get his attention and pointed at my now empty coke bottle. He wasted no time in bringing one over.

"There's someone at the bar who wants to speak to you." He nodded his head towards the few customers congregating there. He didn't need to point him out. It looked like I had been found.

"Send him over." I nodded my head at him, not looking forward to this conversation.

Since the day I'd opened this place, I'd always had one rule in place: control—keep a hold of it. If I lost my patience, I would only damage the business, my reputation and most importantly, my staff. I took the role of business owner seriously, and I promised myself that I would never go back to the Alex I was before this place. That Alex had been an arsehole.

"What can I do for you?" I asked him. I gestured to the stool opposite me, hoping to get this over with.

"I'd like to apologise," he replied. "I'm sorry for the way that I acted last time I was here. I had no right to have a go at you about your relationship with Charlotte."

I looked at him, accepting that he was sorry. He had dark shadows beneath his eyes and it seemed like he hadn't shaved in the last couple of weeks. He looked exhausted.

"That's okay," I said dismissively.

"It's not okay." He waved his hand in a defeating posture. "I had no right to shout at you about Charlotte. I know nothing is going on between you and her."

I tensed. He had a note of disgust in his tone when he emphasised the word 'her', almost as though the idea of her finding someone new was beyond her—almost as though she didn't deserve to find someone new because there couldn't be anyone better than him for her.

"Excuse me?" I asked.

"I don't mean it to sound offensive." He looked up at me. "I just know you and her are only friends." He shook his head at himself. "I can only imagine the things she has told you about me and her."

Me and her.

The fucker was making it really hard for me to keep

hold of that control of mine at the moment. If he kept talking about him and Charlie, it was possible another window was going to get damaged when I threw his body through it.

"She hasn't told me anything." I rested my elbows on the table before crossing my arms. "Just that you're a cheating arsehole." I gave him a big smile, trying to show how bothered I wasn't, even though I obviously was. I expected to hit a nerve, but it just rolled off him.

He looked over to my newly glazed window before cocking an eyebrow at me. "New window?" he asked. The fucker was mocking me now.

"Nothing else to apologise for?" I asked, baiting him.

"Not that I can think of." He shrugged his shoulders before standing. "I had better be going to be honest." He took a few steps away before I spoke up again.

"Scott, help David to the door."

He turned back to look at me.

"You're banned from this day on." I looked back down at my paperwork, not wanting to waste another minute on him. He was the past and the arsehole needed to accept that and move the fuck on.

*F*riday was finally here and I was halfway out the door.

"See you boys later." I grabbed the long-stemmed daisies from where they were lying on the bar and grabbed my tool-kit with my other hand. "Any problems, don't call me," I joked.

"I've never met anyone so excited to change a door lock before," Addie said as she entered the room.

James gave a wolf whistle from behind the bar.

"Damn, woman. Where are you going dressed like that?"

She grinned and gave us a twirl on the spot. She had a sparkly silver dress that came to her mid-thigh, her hair was curled, makeup was done and she had a very high pair of stilettos on her feet. "Thank you." She rolled her eyes at me. "Some of us had to vacate the apartment before Mr. Hot New Bartender Boyfriend arrived." She winked at me and looked over at James. "I'll have a Cosmo please, handsome." She pointed her thumb over her shoulder. "You had best get over there."

I nodded before walking past her, tapping her on the shoulder as I went. "I'll leave your key with Charlie."

"Don't do anything I wouldn't do," she called after me.

I shook my head at her confidence. I didn't think there was anything that she wouldn't do on a date.

Walking up the block, I entered the code Charlie had messaged me a couple of days ago and then knocked on the door, eagerly waiting for her to answer. She didn't keep me waiting long. The sound of the chain being unlatched met my ears before the door opened, revealing her to me.

"Oh, wow." I looked at her, trying to come up with something better to say.

She was barefoot, dressed in a white, flowy summer dress that came to just past her knees.

She giggled at my expression before she waved me in.

"These are for you." I held the flowers out to her. "I know you have some at the shop but now you can have some here."

"They are beautiful, Alex. Thank you." She reached up and kissed my cheek, stepping aside. "I'll go and put them in some water."

"No problem." I set my toolbox on the floor and took a look at the lock. "I'll just get started on this door." I bent down to grab my screwdriver and began undoing the screws. Tossing the old lock on the floor, I made short work of fitting the new brass one. I also replaced the chain lock, not liking how thin and flimsy the previous one looked. It wouldn't have taken much to kick the door open with only that chain for security.

"You've finished already?" she asked when I walked into the kitchen.

"You're all protected now." I grinned at her, loving the way that her eyes trailed over my chest. "Can I smell something cooking? Oh, before I forget, here is a key for your landlord and Addie." I held them out to her, dropping them into her palm.

"Well, I know you mentioned Chinese, but I thought I would cook for us instead. I hope that's okay." She dropped the keys on the worktop.

"Of course." I took a seat at the worktop, watching her stir the sauce. "So, what are you cooking?"

"My famous BBQ chicken melts." She leaned over and placed a bottle of Budweiser in front of me. "Is that okay?"

"Come here." I turned my body to the side and held my arm out, waving her closer to me.

She took my hand and fitted her body in between my legs.

"I'm guessing that David made you a question a lot of things. Didn't he?" I dipped my head to catch her gaze, sensing she was trying to avoid my eyes.

"I messed up, didn't I?" she asked. It came out as a whisper and I knew that my question had put her on the spot.

I didn't want to make her feel like she was backed into a corner, but I didn't want us to lie to each other. Honesty was the only way we could do this. "You didn't." I shook my head before lifting our hands and linking them around my neck. "I'm not him, though, okay? Whatever went wrong in the past, let's leave it there."

She frowned at me and I knew that she was reading my words.

I wasn't sure if I wanted her to read me. "I will never try and control you the way that he did," I vowed. It was a promise that I would never break. I'd never had someone make me want to be a good guy, but the way that she was staring at me meant I wanted to keep it that way.

"Something happened in your past, didn't it?" she asked.

I looked at her, hating that question.

"What happened in your past, Alex?" she asked, reading me right. Her beautiful eyes shone into mine, waiting for my answer. "You can talk to me. I don't judge people." She seemed so open and honest. Her eyes were asking me to trust her.

I wanted to trust her—I *did* trust her—but there was a small part of me deep down inside that was afraid she would judge. Everyone judged a book by its cover. They couldn't help it. It was instinct.

She tensed at my silence before she pulled away from me.

I knew I had hurt her with my silence. I knew that she expected me to open up to her like she had opened up to me.

I latched my hands on to her hips, stopping her

from moving away. "Hold on. I'm sorry. I don't usually talk about myself with women," I said hesitantly. I shrugged my shoulders. It was ironic that I was the one now feeling backed up into a corner. "It's not pretty," I said, shaking my head.

She stepped away from me, stopping at the stove on the other side of the worktop. She turned the dials off and came back to me, holding her hand out. "Let's talk."

"What about dinner?" I asked, taking her hand.

"You're more important than dinner." She led me through the lounge and into her bedroom, sitting on the end of her bed and pulling me down next to her. "We can be alone in here if Addie comes home. Talk to me." She turned to the side, resting her kneecaps against the outside of my thigh. "I promise I won't judge."

CHAPTER

Ten

Charlie

ension. I had seen it reflected back at me so many times since David and I had broken up. However, this was the first time I had ever seen Alex looking anything other than calm and laidback. He usually appeared as though he didn't have a worry in the world. That was *not* the man that I was currently looking at.

"This isn't how I imagined tonight going." He chuckled, trying to inject some light-heartedness but it wasn't working. "I thought tonight would be a little more chilled than this."

"If you don't want to tell me, I will understand." I was trying to be comforting but I didn't think it was working. I wanted him to talk to me. I wanted him to trust me enough to talk to me about his problems. More importantly than that, though, I just wanted him to be comfortable enough to trust me enough to share in his concerns.

"You're the first woman that has ever expressed enough interest in wanting to talk to me about my past." He rubbed his thumb along my knuckles. "Usually, it's just sex and then we go back to our own lives." He turned to me, his fingers tightening on mine briefly before letting go. "Can we lie down?" he asked.

I nodded, shuffling up the bed, laying on my side and turning to face him. He copied my movements, mirroring my position and placing his hand on my hip, resting it there before taking a deep breath.

"You might want to throw me out of here when I'm finished," he joked.

"It's a good job I have a good lock on my door then," I teased.

He chuckled before resting his head more comfortably on the pillow. "Okay, uh..." He sighed. "When I was younger, I didn't live in a great place."

"Oh." Damn it. I had to push him, didn't I?

"Yeah. In my house, it was pretty normal for a mother to wear bruises. Dad had his good days, but he also had a lot of bad days. The closer I got to the age where I would be leaving home and going to college, the more the bruises would appear on her. It was going from a weekly occurrence to more of an every other day thing."

"Alex, I am so sorry."

He was looking at me but I didn't think he was seeing me any longer. He was trapped in his head—stuck in memories of his past.

"I'd gone to visit Manchester College the weekend before I was scheduled to leave. I was going to be studying Business and Finance." His hand tensed on my hip. "I went home, and my father wasn't there. James was sitting next to my mother and I... Her face was completely covered in bruises. She was broken."

"Alex..." His eyes were glistening and he was breaking my heart.

"I'd always protected James from it—or I thought I had at least. When I saw him look at her, I could see the cracks forming in him. He'd worshipped our mother. He was always a mummy's boy. I used to tease him about it." He chuckled but it sounded hollow. His eyes came back to mine before he shook his head at himself.

It almost seemed as though he was trying to shake the memories away.

"Many times I tried to intervene. She would always stop me, though—always said that she could handle it and to keep my nose out. I listened to her because she always made it seem like it was normal—that it happened in every house. How sad is that?"

"She sounds like a strong woman," I said.

"She was. She was bright and funny, sweet, caring and always had a hug waiting."

"Was?" I asked. Was. Past tense.

"Dad came home and he didn't know I was there. He had been drinking heavily and came back shouting abuse at her. I think she had it worse when I wasn't there."

"What happened?" I whispered.

"I came back into the room just in time to see him push her over and punch James in the face. He went down, hitting the corner of his forehead on the edge of the table." He blew out a breath before lying on his back. "I lost it."

He sounded so cold.

"I threw myself at him. I punched him in the face a few times but I..." He lifted his hand and placed it on his forehead. "I didn't stop hitting him. James pulled me off him but he..." He shook his head. "By the time the paramedics arrived, he was dead. I was arrested and I spent the next six years in jail."

"Oh, Alex." I couldn't imagine the man at my side killing anyone. I knew that he must still carry the guilt with him and I knew that it must have been scarily violent for it to get to that stage. For him to take a life. "What happened to your mum?" I asked.

"She became an alcoholic. James found her when I was three years into my sentence. She had a heart attack and died in her sleep." He turned his head to look at me. "I think this is the part where you throw me out of your life and ask me never to come back."

I reached over and stroked my fingers down his cheek. "You don't know me that well if you think that of me."

He placed his hand over mine before pulling it to his lips. "I don't deserve you," he whispered.

"None of us are saints, Alex." I gave him a faint smile. "You saved your mum. James, too. He would have killed her if you had gone off to college. He had obviously already started trying to make James his victim as well."

"I'm not a hero, Charlie." His hand tensed on mine.

"I don't want a saint, Alex," I defended. "All I want is your trust, honesty and for you to never stop looking at me like that."

"Like what?" he whispered.

"Like I'm the only woman that you see."

Confidence and Charlie never usually went together but after tonight, listening to him pour his heart and broken past out to me, I knew that after tonight, we would be stronger. He was a fighter and I would never let him think any less of himself.

"Kiss me," I whispered. I placed my hands on the back of his neck and pulled him down to me.

He leaned over me and softly parted my lips before stroking his tongue against mine.

"I want you," he whispered. He tilted his head and

trailed his tongue down the column of my neck before nibbling on my collarbone. He reached down and slid my dress up my legs, not stopping until he was grasping the outside of my thigh. "Do you want me to stop?"

I looked up at him. I needed to know that I was making the right decision. I needed to know that this was for longer than just one night.

"Do you have protection?" I asked.

He nodded his head.

"A sure thing, am I?" I looked past him, feeling like I was making it too easy for him.

"Don't do that," he whispered. "I just told you more than I have ever told another living soul. You're more than one night for me."

I nodded before trailing my hands down to his belt and slowly unbuckled it.

He dipped his head and he kissed along my shoulder. He moved the straps down until they were hanging off my naked shoulders and slid his hands beneath me and undid the tie at the back of my waist.

I grabbed the back of his neck and pushed him back so that he was on his knees. I positioned my body over his and pulled my arms free of the straps. I pulled the dress down, baring my breasts to him.

"Ah, fuck." He reached down and grasped my breasts, roughly squeezing them in his palms.

I reached for the bottom of his t-shirt and pulled it

up his body. I rocked my hips against his, feeling his hard length against me.

He took over and yanked his t-shirt up and over his head before he threw it behind me. He stared up at me and lowered his head, pressing his forehead against my chest.

"What is it?" I asked. I reached my hands up and laced my fingers through the back of his hair. "What's wrong?"

"Nothing." He shook his head before I felt his breath against my skin. "I thought you would have thrown me out of here by now after what I told you."

I took his face in my hands. I was realising tonight how false the self-confidence was. I could see now that what he wore was a mask for the whole world to see.

"You still carry that day with you, don't you?" I looked at him, feeling like I was seeing him in his true colours for the first time. "You still carry them with you."

"I killed someone, Charlie. That isn't something that you can just move on from."

"I wish that you could," I whispered. I dipped my head and kissed his temple. "I wish that I could make it better for you—help you like you have helped me."

"You do," he whispered. He leaned forwards and pressed his lips to mine before he slid his hands up my thighs. "I want you." He grasped the elastic of my knickers and began roughly pulling them down and I lifted my hips for him, gasping when he ripped my dress down from around my waist with them. "Now."

I nodded before leaning back, placing my head on the pillow.

"You should always be like this," he whispered. "Naked and at my mercy."

He climbed off the bed and unbuckled his jeans. He took a condom out of his pocket, holding it between his teeth before pulling his jeans off and kicking them to the side.

Fuck me, he was big.

He tore the wrapper open and sheathed it over his length. He climbed up the bed, stopping at my ankle. He lowered his head and kissed my skin before he began peppering little kisses up my leg, going straight past where I needed him the most before stopping and sucking my nipple into his mouth.

I spread my legs wider for him, trying to make it comfortable for his large frame.

"I want you," he whispered. "I have wanted you for so fucking long."

I laced my arms around his neck, smiling when he rested his forehead against mine. "I'm sorry I kept you waiting for so long, Alex." I tilted my head and kissed him, parting my lips and moaning when he thrust his tongue into my mouth.

He slid his hand beneath my neck, fusing our mouths together in firmer strokes. He pulled back suddenly before leaning his weight on his hands on either side of me.

"You were worth every minute." He reached down and grasped himself before sliding inside of me.

We both gasped as he entered me.

He moved inside me slowly several times before speeding up. I reached down and grasped his arse cheeks, pulling him against me harder. The action caused him to move further inside me. He pulled back, thrusting inside me roughly again, repeating the action, and I could feel my muscles squeeze him. It wasn't going to take long if he kept going.

He reached down and took my chin, roughly taking my lips. He groaned against them and it sounded so fucking sexy.

"You feel so good," I whispered.

He leaned back on his knees, pulling me with him so that I was over him. "Show me," he whispered. He tightened his arm around my waist before he began lifting me roughly and slamming his hips upwards. "Show me how good it feels." His teeth bit into my neck, causing me to moan.

"Ah, fuck. Like that." I placed my hands on his shoulders, digging my nails in before thrusting my hips against him. "Just like that." I tilted my head back, feeling the pleasure claim me.

After a few more hard thrusts, and I could feel myself begin to tighten around him.

His arm moved around me before he pushed us back down. He grabbed my thigh and wrapped it higher around his waist and slammed his hips against me. He moaned against my mouth before I felt his orgasm hit him.

"Fuck," he whispered. He rolled onto his back, pulling me with him. "Fuck." He leaned down and kissed the top of my head.

"You said that already," I giggled. "You sound fucked," I mocked.

"Royally fucked." He winked at me, pulling me down on his chest. "Completely."

CHAPTER
Eleven

Alex

ooking down, I smiled when I saw that Charlie was still beside me. She had her face cuddled into my arm with the cutest pout on her face. It was almost seven am, so I was surprised she was still in bed. She usually opened up at ten am, but the time it took to bake all of her products meant that she'd normally be in the kitchen from six or seven am onwards.

I leaned over to pull the sheet around her as she had goose bumps travelling up her arm. I couldn't tell if it was from my touch or whether it was because she was cold. Placing it over her shoulder, I smiled when she cuddled herself closer to me. I lifted my arm and rested my head down on hers. I relaxed back against her mattress, feeling content enough to fall back to sleep. Before I could, though, reality crashed back into us, popping our little bubble.

BANG! BANG!

A sound woke Charlie and most likely, half of the building.

"Shhh. It's okay." I swung my legs out of bed and grabbed my jeans, pulling them on. "It's probably Addie."

She nodded at me, looking uncertain. Her hair was rumpled and it made her look like a sex kitten, and I looked forward to rumpling it all over again.

"Open this door! I know you're in there," David's voice thundered from the door.

Her eyes widened in shock as she grasped the blanket, holding it tightly over her chest.

"Stay here," I ordered. I sounded like a prick talking to her like that, but I wasn't having her anywhere near that arsehole. I fastened my jeans before buckling my belt, ignoring the second round of bangs that came from the main door.

"I know you're there, Charlie. I just want to talk to you. I checked the shop and you're not there..." The handle twisted, rattling the door. "Just open the door, Charlie."

Oh, this was going to be fun.

I took a breath before opening the door, and his face dropped when he saw me before his fist shot out, connecting with my jaw. "You fucking bastard!" he shouted at me, the force of his punch knocking me backwards.

I grabbed onto the wall, refusing to go down. The fucker had a strong punch on him, I'd give him that.

"David, no!" Charlie shrieked. She came running out of her bedroom with the sheet wrapped around her body. "Stop it!"

"You slut!" he shouted, turning on her. "You let this prick in between your legs? Were you fucking him when we were together?"

"Hey!" I shouted angrily. I fucking hated the way that she cowered at his words. "Don't talk to her like that!"

"He's a fucking bar owner, Charlie. You're just another notch on his belt!"

Her shoulders slumped at his words and I knew a part of what he was saying to her was hitting beneath her armour.

"I said"—I grabbed his shoulder and spun him back to face me—"don't talk to her like that!" My fist shot out, connecting with his jaw. My temper was on a leash, and he was making it damn fucking difficult to keep it in check.

He went down on his hands and knees before he spat blood out on to the hardwood floor.

Charlie ran to him, bending down and lowering her hand to help him up. She had an angelic quality about her, but at that moment, she was bending to a devil—a devil who didn't fucking deserve anything from her.

"Get away from me, you slut!" He smacked her hand away from him before he climbed to his feet and stomped to the door. "You'll regret this."

"You cheated on her, arsehole!" I yelled after him. "You lost her a long fucking time ago!"

I hated the way that Charlie jumped at my words, but there was no fucking way I was going to stand there and watch her take his bullshit.

He continued walking, slamming the door and leaving us to it.

"Well," I sighed, "that wasn't really how I imagined this morning playing out." I reached my hand out to stroke her arm but before I could reach her, she turned away from me and walked back towards her bedroom.

"I'm going to take a shower," she muttered. She said it loud enough for me to hear, but I had a feeling it wasn't an open offer for me to join her. Shaking my head, I walked into the kitchen and began mixing some pancake mix. After making a decent stack, I headed to the bedroom to grab my t-shirt. I froze in the doorway when I saw Charlie sitting on the end of the bed.

She was already dressed in her works t-shirt and leggings. Her hair was knotted on the top of her head and tucked off her neck. She looked fucking gorgeous, apart from the fact that she seemed like she was close to crying.

"Are you okay?" I asked.

"He called me a slut," she whispered. She wiped her hand across her cheek and I knew that she was already crying. "You're the first guy I've been with since him and I..."

I sighed, taking a seat next to her. "You don't have to explain yourself." I slid my arm around her shoulders and pulled her into me. "That fucker has just realised that he's lost. He was lashing out. That's all."

"You don't believe that," she whispered. She turned her eyes up to me, reading me right.

"No, I don't." I leaned my head down and kissed her lips before pulling back. "Until I have proof that he was the one sneaking in here, though, there's not much we can do."

"I know." She looked past me to the open doorway. "Did you make us pancakes?" She pasted a small smile on her face, attempting to lighten things up a little.

"I did." I grinned at her before standing up and holding my hand out to her. "Only the best for my lady."

She giggled as I led her out the door, allowing me to pull a seat out for her.

"This is different." She placed her clasped hands on the table, playing along. "It's usually the other way around."

I placed the stack of pancakes in between us. "Are you a honey or a sugar fan?" I grinned down at her.

Instead of reaching for the honey, I moved the sugar bowl closer to her.

"You know me well," she teased.

I watched her sprinkle sugar over her pancake, chuckling when she wrinkled her nose at the jar of honey. I reached over and offered a raspberry to her. She took it from my grasp, nibbling it before leaning forward and pressing her lips to mine.

I hummed against her mouth, tasting the juice from her lips. "Fuck, that's sweet."

She giggled before spearing a bit of pancake and feeding me with her fork. "This is nice," she whispered.

"What is? Feeding me?" I grinned. "I like it, too."

"No!" She giggled once more. "This is." She reached across and took my hand in hers. "Being close to you."

"I'm assuming this didn't happen when you were with David." I rubbed my thumb along her knuckles, trying to take the sting out of my words with my touch.

She sighed. "A lot didn't happen when I was with David." She sounded so despondent that I had to ask the next question.

"Did he ever hurt you?" I stared into her eyes, wanting her to see that I wasn't judging. Just like she didn't judge me.

"No." She shook her head. "He never laid a hand against me. He...He wasn't 'boyfriend of the year' sometimes, but I guess I can't have been the easiest partner to have, either." She shrugged her shoulders. "When your partner goes elsewhere for sexual gratification," she mocked, "it's never a good thing."

"Nothing wrong with the sexual gratification you offer as far as I can see," I joked, wanting to lighten the storm that I could see brewing in her eyes. "You're not to blame for his issues."

She nodded at me before her eyes flicked past me to the clock hanging on the kitchen wall. "I need to get going." She wiped her lips before standing up. "Will I see you later?"

"I suppose I can be seen with you," I joked. "I'll stay here and wash the dishes and I'll come by and see you this afternoon."

"I look forward to it." She leaned up to kiss my lips before she was dashing out the door.

I wasted no time in filling the sink with bubbles, rinsing the dishes before popping them in the dishwasher. It had become a long-used habit of mine to rinse dishes before putting them in the dishwasher. James called it obsessive but he was a messy fucker compared to me.

Opening the main door, I froze when I heard the landline ring. I waited a few moments, nosily seeing who was calling her. After a few rings, a beep sounded, identifying that the answering machine had kicked in. Seconds later, a voice rang out, shattering the silence of the apartment.

"Charlie, it's me." David. "I need to see you. I'm sorry about this morning. I handled it wrongly. Come to me. I'll be at The Glass Eye at two this afternoon. Please. Once you hear what I have to say, I know you will understand."

The call ended, and so did my patience. That fucker had just fried my last nerve.

Walking down the block, my mind was six hours ahead of me. That arsehole was playing mind games with her. He was trying to corner her—make her feel something for him. After this morning, when I'd watched her cower at his words, I knew that outbursts like that weren't a new thing for her. She had been too calm during it. He may not have hurt her physically, but I saw first-hand what shouting at someone and belittling them every day could do to a person's self-esteem. It destroyed them from the inside out and there was no way in hell that I was going to just stand there and allow him to spin his games on her.

There was no way that I was going to lose her to a piece of filth like him.

The day passed slowly and then the deadline approached.

"Are you going to tell me what the problem is?" James asked, tossing the rag on the bar in front of me. "You have been away with the fairies all day."

"David turned up at Charlie's place this morning.

He called her a slut." I shook my head regretfully. "I may have hit him."

"Of course you did," he replied. "Is she okay?"

"As well as she can be. I don't think this is the first time that he has ever gone off on her like that." I ground my teeth, hating the idea of her putting up with that. "Why would she do that?" I asked, voicing my thoughts. "Why would she allow it?"

"There's a fine line between love and hate, bro." He cleaned a glass, focusing on it instead of me. "Mum loved Dad, but I think there were times where she hated him as well." He looked at me. "Did you tell her about...?"

"I did, yeah. She took it better than I thought she would." I stood, tucking the stool in closer to the bar. "I'm going to go."

"Is this a good idea?" he asked, knowing full well where I was going. "She might not understand."

"I don't care right now. This has happened before on my watch." I walked to the door, resigned to my decision. "I'm not losing Charlie to the same mind-fuck game that I lost Mum to." I didn't mention the voice message he'd left on the machine. I knew James would only read too much into it. He would tell me to butt out and insist that it wasn't any of my business. He would probably be right, but the way I was feeling... I didn't want to think about it.

Walking into The Glass Eye, I looked around, trying

to find him. I didn't want to do this publicly, but I also wasn't going to just sit back and watch him dig his claws back into Charlie. Spotting him, I didn't stop until I was pulling a seat out in front of him. Sitting down, I leaned back, secretly gloating on the inside at the look of panic on his face.

He quickly wiped it off before his face morphed into an icy mask. "What do you want?" he asked. "I have a meeting in a few minutes."

"She's not coming," I said coldly.

"So she sent you, did she?" he asked. He curled his lip in disgust, before reaching for his glass of scotch. He knocked it back before loudly tapping it back down on the table. "Couldn't come here and answer to me herself, could she?"

"She doesn't need to answer to you." I said it slowly because he needed to get the fucking message. "She has a new life now, David. *You* are the one that fucked this up. *You* are the one that cheated on her and *you* are the one that thinks it's okay to speak to your woman like a piece of shit."

"What the fuck do you know?" he slurred. "I know that you think you know her but you don't know fuck all. You don't know her."

"You're right," I agreed. "I don't know every little thing about your relationship with her and you know what? I don't need to." I stood up and took a small step away. "It's time for you to let go now, David." I tucked my hands into my jean pockets. "I don't want to see you hanging around her building anymore." I raised my eyebrows at him. "This is me asking nicely. I won't ask again."

I turned around and walked away, leaving him with his alcohol and hopefully, down a path that was far away from us.

CHAPTER
Twelve

Charlie

It had been several days since I had last seen
Alex. It didn't worry me, but he had been
oddly quiet lately. I hoped that would change tonight. It
was Thursday evening, and I was hoping to convince
him to come around to mine if he wasn't working at the
bar. Addie was out with friends, which meant that I
would be all by my lonesome.

Climbing the stairs, I dialled Alex's number, feeling
the tiredness of the day seeping into my bones. Curling
up with him on my sofa sounded like the perfect ending
to my day.

"Hey, darling," his voice echoed down the line.
"How was your day?"

"It was okay. I'm just getting home and I—" I approached my door, freezing at what I saw.

The word 'SLUT' was graffitied in a vertical line down my door.

"Hello? Charlie?" Alex asked at my silence. "Are you still there?"

"I'm here," I choked out. "Alex, I need you."

"I'm on my way." Seconds before he hung up, he said to James, "I've got to go. Watch the bar."

Tears stung my eyes, but I didn't want to break out here in my corridor. I didn't want to break at all. I wanted to be better than that. I slid the key in the lock and walked inside. I left the door open and headed to the kitchen, grabbing the bottle of wine from the fridge that I had tucked away. Uncorking it, I filled a large glass before taking a seat on the worktop and waited for Alex to arrive.

I heard him running up the stairs and several moments later, I heard him.

"What the fuck?" he muttered. "Charlie?"

"In here," I called. "Come and join me for a drink." I took a large gulp of wine before looking up.

He came around the corner and I could see the anger that was coursing through him was written all over his face. He didn't even try and hide it.

"I'm going to fucking kill him." He stormed back to the door.

I jumped in surprise when I heard the door slam

closed. I put my glass down next to the half-empty bottle and hopped down, going to check on him. I half-expected him to have left and been on his way to see David. Instead, he was by the door.

"Hey," I whispered. "It's okay." It wasn't okay but I needed to calm him down.

"It isn't okay," he ground out. His hands tensed where he was holding the door frame. "He is lucky I am not ripping him apart right now." The muscles in his back bunched and I knew that he was keeping a tight grip on his temper.

"Is that what you want to do?" I asked. I reached over, closing the gap between us and stroked my fingers down the centre of his back. "You're angry."

"I'm fucking furious." His words sounded calm but the punch he delivered to the back of the door was anything but. If he'd hit the wall, I imagine he would have put a hole through the plaster.

I took a step closer and laid my head against his back. His heart was thumping at a fast pace.

"Why are you still here?" I asked, needing to know. "I want to know. How are you keeping so calm because I want to...?"

"Because of you." He sighed, reaching his arm behind him and resting his hand on my lower back. "If I do what I want to that piece of filth—if I let the monster out—I will lose you." He turned around suddenly and took my face in his hands. "And I am just not ready for that to happen."

"I want you," I whispered. I reached up, biting his earlobe before soothing it with my tongue. "I know you want me." I reached down and rubbed him over his trousers. I grinned when I felt him harden at my touch.

"Careful, Charlie." He roughly grabbed me by my upper arms and pushed me back a little. He glared down at me. "You do *not* want me when I'm like this."

"You won't hurt me," I whispered. I leaned up and licked his bottom lip. I needed him to want to fuck me as much as I wanted him to. "I'm already broken, Alex. You can't hurt me."

"You want me to fuck you, do you?" He spun me around and pressed me against him. He rocked against me, sliding his hand down over my stomach and between my legs, rubbing me over my leggings.

"Yes." I grabbed his wrist and rubbed his hand harder against me. "I want you to fuck me." I reached back and slid my fingers into his hair. I moaned again when his teeth bit down where my neck met my shoulder. "I want you to break me." I bit his bottom lip before thrusting my tongue in between his parted lips. "I want you to own me."

That was it.

He spun me around and grabbed my upper thighs before lifting me up. "Wrap those legs around me." He tapped my left arse cheek before he grasped them both in his hands and marched me into my bedroom. "You will probably regret this in the morning." He kicked the door shut and lowered me to the floor at the foot of my bed. He dropped to his knees in front of me and grabbed the waistband of my leggings. He yanked them down over my hips, kissing across my stomach. He pulled them down to my knees, and I toppled backward onto my bed as he pulled my shoes off, tossing them to the corner of the room and continuing to rip my leggings and knickers off.

I scooted backwards, straightening my legs out to help him pull them off faster, and he reached up, fisting his t-shirt before pulling it up and over his head.

Climbing up on the bed, he spread my legs wider, yanking me closer to him. He smirked up at me before his mouth moved down on me. I gasped when he stroked his tongue up the centre of my pussy before he sucked my clit. His tongue moved fast, not giving me time to become accustomed to having his mouth on me.

"Oh, oh fuck." My arms gave way and my head crashed to the mattress. I arched my back, letting the pleasure he was giving me take over my body.

"Off," he mumbled against me, moving my t-shirt up my body. The noise sent sparks through me.

"Off!" he said again, this time smacking the outside of my thigh lightly with his order. He grabbed my wrists and helped pull my upper body up.

I groaned, grabbing the sides of my t-shirt and

pulling it up over my head. I threw it to the side on the floor before slumping back down.

Alex flicked his tongue down lower, moving it inside of me. He reached up and rubbed his fingers over my clit. He did it again and I felt him groan against me. "Come for me, darling." He spread my legs wider, digging his fingers into my hips. "Now." He sucked me harder then reached up and grasped my breast roughly.

I arched my back, moaning, calling out his name as I came for him and gasped when I felt him move back from me. I expected him to give me time to recover but I wasn't getting that.

"That was different." I gasped, trying to calm my breathing.

"That was nothing, darling." He closed my legs before he grabbed me by my hips and flipped me over on to my front.

"Wh-what are you doing?" I asked.

He crawled over me and I felt the rough fabric of his jeans scratch against the side of my naked legs. He dipped his head and licked the column of my neck, grabbing my hair in a ponytail before tilting my head back. He leaned his face over mine and kissed me, our mouths upside down over each other's.

He pulled back after a moment before he moved down my body. Seconds later, I heard the sound of a tear and his groans filling the room.

"Aren't you going to take your jeans off?" I looked over my shoulder, giving him a pointed look.

"Fuck no." He smacked my arse cheek before he lifted my hips, bringing me closer to where he needed me. "I need to fuck you." He reached down to grasp himself before he slid himself inside me.

"That feels n—"

Before I could finish my sentence, he slammed his hips forward, impaling me on his cock roughly.

"Oh, fuck!" I shrieked. I placed my palms on the mattress, supporting my weight on them.

Reaching down, he pulled my hair back, tightening it around his fist before he moved his other hand down and unclasped my bra. The straps fell down my arms, exposing my naked breasts to the air. He reached down and grasped them in his hands before pulling me back against him so that I was kneeling. He pressed his chest against my back as he continued to roughly pump himself in and out of me.

Fuck me, he was big. He seemed a lot bigger in this position.

"I love your filthy fucking moans." He reached up and placed his hand around my throat before I felt his lips against my cheek. "You're like my own wet fucking dream." He trailed his hand down between my breasts before moving further down my stomach. "Don't keep me waiting," he whispered. He took my chin and turned my face to his, thrusting his tongue into my mouth, tongue-fucking me like his hips were. "Come for me." He pinched my clit in between his fingers before rubbing it fast. "Come for me, Charlie."

He slammed his hips forwards, pulling back and repeating the action. He grasped my breast, pinching and pulling my nipple before I came apart, my inner muscles squeezing him.

Moments later, he thrust a few more times and I felt him come inside the condom, groaning my name into my neck. He slowly moved us forwards, pulling out of me and laying us down on our sides so that we were spooning.

After a few moments, I placed my hand on top of his where it was resting against my hip.

"I feel fucked." I gasped before letting a giggle escape.

"Well, you did ask." He chuckled, leaning over me and softly kissed my lips. He climbed off the bed, pulling the condom off and tying a knot in it. He tossed it in the bin before he began walking to the door.

"Do you have to go?" I asked. I wrapped the blanket around me, not really wanting to flash Addie if she was home.

"I'll just go and call James to cover the rest of my shift." He took his phone out of his pocket before looking back at me. "Do you have any of those caramel bites here?"

I rolled my eyes at his shameful begging. "Check the

fridge." I had created a monster when it came to my desserts. I reached over and pulled a strappy top on before escaping to the bathroom to clean up. Pulling on a clean pair of pyjama bottoms, I went to the kitchen, feeling my stomach start to growl and pulled the drawer open that housed all the many takeaway menus, feeling his arms wrap around me.

"What are we having?" he asked.

I hummed before answering. "Depends what you're hungry for."

He growled under his breath before he trailed his nose up the column of my neck. "I know what I'm hungry for," he whispered.

I gasped, surprised. "Seriously? After that? I thought I had worn you out."

"You wish." He pulled the hair back from my neck. "The only thing I'm hungry for is you."

I giggled. "I thought you wanted the caramel bites," I teased. I turned around and slid my arms up around his neck.

"I couldn't find them." He leaned down and kissed my lips, sucking on my bottom lip. "I would much rather have you instead." He pulled back, his face sobering before he spoke again. "Do you want me to come around and paint over your door?"

I shook my head immediately. "No. I will report it to the landlord and the police."

He raised his eyebrows at me. "Are you sure about

that?" He rubbed his thumb along my hip bone beneath my t-shirt.

"Yes." I nodded my head. "This isn't the David that I once knew. I want to help him."

"Okay," he sighed. He dipped his head to kiss me, but before he could, I reached up and placed my finger over his lips.

"Will you come with me?" I asked. "I thought I'd report it to the landlord tonight and then we could go to the station tomorrow."

"Sure." He held his hand out for the menus. "Why don't you go and ring him and I'll order us some food?"

"Thank you, Alex." I handed the menus to him and grabbed my phone, dialling the landlord's number and filling him in on the latest dramatic episode in my life.

CHAPTER Thirteen

Alex

After taking a bus to the police station that was based more in the centre of the city, I took Charlie's hand in mine, attempting to ease her stress. She hadn't slept the best last night and I knew that she was still feeling uneasy about this—about what she was minutes away from doing.

"You okay?" I asked. I looked down at her, needing to check in with her.

"Nervous." She chuckled and I could hear how tense she sounded.

"I know." Before I could say anything more, my phone rang, disturbing us. "What?" I asked, answering James.

"Where are you?" he asked. The clink of glasses sounded down the line before Scott's laughter joined it.

"I told you," I snapped. "Me and Charlie are going to the police station to—" I stopped talking when I looked ahead of us. We were only a block away from the station and the sight in front of me had me freezing.

"Alex?" Charlie asked, turning her face up to me. Her fingers tensed around mine. "What is it?" She turned her head to follow my line of sight. David was standing outside, leaning on a wall. A couple of police officers were with him, and I knew that whatever we had planned for today had just gone up in smokes. David had done something.

The officers turned to face Charlie and me when David nodded his head.

"Get down to the station, James," I ordered. "Lisbon Road. Now." I quickly hung up and slipped my phone in the arse pocket of Charlie's jeans.

"Alex, you're scaring me," she whispered.

"It's okay, my darling." I lifted our clasped hands and pressed my lips to the back of hers. "Just stay calm."

The police officer approached us, looking official. Whatever it was, I knew that it was serious enough to have the officers facing me and Charlie instead of the sleazebag they had just left.

"Mr. Winters?" the male officer on the left asked.

He was tall and skinny but had a polite expression on his face.

I nodded my head. "Is there a problem, officer?" I stared past them, glaring at the cocky smirk that appeared on David's face.

"We have had a complaint that you attacked this gentleman over my shoulder."

"What?" Charlie shrieked. She looked at David before going back to the officer. "That's a lie!"

"We have a statement that the marks on Mr. Smith's face were from an altercation with you at his girlfriend's address."

This just kept getting better, didn't it?

"That's bullshit!" Charlie shouted, getting angry. "Who is this girlfriend?"

The officer looked down at the notepad in his hand.

"A Miss Charlotte Chase."

"Are you fucking high?" Charlie shouted at David before looking back at the officer. "*I'm* Charlotte Chase. David and I separated just short of a year ago." She sounded like she was going to burst into tears. "I had a break-in at my apartment and wanted the locks changed. Alex was kind enough to do it and he..." She hesitated, staring down at the floor before straightening her shoulders and looking back up at the officers. "He stayed the night. The following morning, David came around to my apartment. He called me a slut and that's when things got out of hand. He frightened me a little and Alex punched him in the face."

"Would you be willing to make a statement testifying to that, Miss Chase?" He looked down at her, waiting patiently for her response.

I hated that she was under this pressure. I rubbed my thumb over her knuckles.

She looked at David before nodding her head. "Yes."

The officers separated: one to handle David and the other walked Charlie and me into the station.

"Miss Chase, if you'll just step in here." He held a door to an investigation room open, giving her a polite smile.

"Can Alex come in?" she asked. She had a tight grip on my hand, showing me how much she was struggling.

"I'm afraid not." He shook his head. "He is welcome to wait here," he said, waving his hand to a bench of seats that were situated against the wall.

"It's okay, darling." I let her hand go and rested mine on the bottom of her spine. "I'll wait here. It's going to be okay."

She gave me a small smile and I fucking hated how watery her eyes looked.

I took a seat on the bench, clenching my hands into a fist repeatedly. I was close to losing my fucking shit, and I knew that it wasn't going to take much for me to completely lose it. David was trying to drive a wedge between Charlie and me. He wanted me to be arrested today. He—just like I didn't—never expected Charlie to step up. She was a strong woman, but I'd underestimated her. She'd surprised me today, and I knew that she had also surprised herself.

Looking at my watch, I sighed when I saw that she had been in there for over thirty minutes. I stood up to go and ring James from the payphone when the door to the interview room opened and out walked my girl—my girl who had been fucking crying going by the redness on her cheeks.

I glared at the police officer, not appreciating that he had obviously pushed her fucking buttons—too many of the fuckers if this is what he had done to her.

I took her face in my hands. I didn't bother asking her if she was okay. It was fucking clear that she wasn't.

"Take me home," she whispered.

Home. Not to the shop but home.

I nodded at her, wrapping my arm around her shoulders before tucking her into my side. We were halfway down the block before we were interrupted by the officer arsehole stopping us.

"We will be in touch, Miss Chase."

She nodded before turning her head and hiding her face into my arm.

I didn't appreciate the way that he was staring at her. It was true that I didn't like *any* man looking at her but fuck... Right now he was looking at her like he knew more than I did. It was clear that whatever she had told him in that room it was shit that she had refused to tell me about.

Walking into the waiting room near the exit, we stopped when we saw James sitting there. He stood up when he saw us and came straight over.

"Is everything okay?" He frowned down at Charlie before he hugged her. "Your phone call scared the shit out of me."

"We're fine." I rubbed my hand up and down her arm. "We just need to get Charlie home." I gave him a pointed look over her head, urging him to catch on and help me get her the fuck out of here.

He nodded, leading the way to the exit and holding the door open for us as we passed him.

We all piled into James's car that was parked at the kerb with Charlie sitting in the passenger seat. As we got closer to her apartment building, James looked in his rear-view mirror, questioning me with his eyes about what the fuck was happening.

I shook my head at him, climbing out of the car when he came to a stop. I helped Charlie from the car and steered her to the door. Before we could go through it, she turned to face down the block to where our bar and her café shop was.

"I should go and close the shop," she whispered. "Addie is there all on her own."

"James will do it," I said, butting in.

"Of course." He nodded his head. "I'll take care of it. Don't worry about it." He turned away and walked down the block, leaving his car outside the apartment building where it sat.

We silently climbed the stairs before she led us inside, tossing her keys on the worktop and placing my phone down next to it.

"Do you mind if I go and have a lie-down?" she asked, turning to face me.

"You go on in, darling." I rubbed my fingers down her arm before giving her hand a gentle squeeze.

She nodded and walked to her bedroom, toeing her shoes off before laying down on her bed. She lay on her side and faced away from me.

I closed her door gently and walked to the kitchen. Picking my phone off the counter, I dialled James's number but stopped when I heard the front door open. I walked over, positioning myself in the line of view to warn James to be quiet so as not to disturb Charlie.

Instead, Addie's worried face met mine. James walked in behind her.

"Where is she?" she asked. Her eyes flicked to Charlie's closed bedroom door before coming back to me. She crossed her arms before she spoke again. "What happened?"

I nodded my head to the kitchen, leading the way back in the direction I came from.

"I'm serious, Alex. Don't fob me off. What. Happened?"

"David reported me to the police. Said that I had assaulted him at his girlfriend's apartment." I looked over Addie's head at James, nodding my head at the look of shock that was on his face.

"Are you fucking kidding me?" She looked at James. "Did you know about this?"

I raised my eyebrows in surprise, noting the way she spoke to him. So familiar. Something was going on there.

"No!" He raised his hands in surrender. "Fuck. I would have told you if I knew..."

Definitely something going on.

"Charlie had to make a statement. She was a bit emotional when she came out of the interrogation room." I looked at Addie, wanting to see any sign that she may be hiding something from me. "She's lying in her room now."

"I had better go and see her." She turned away from me, but I stopped her before she could get too far.

"Hold up." I walked around her and placed myself in front of her. "First, you're going to tell me."

She looked up at me, and I knew that by the expression on her face I wasn't going to like whatever was going to come out of her mouth next.

"Tell you what?" she asked. Her voice came out as a whisper.

"Whatever it is that I don't know." I crossed my arms. I was trying my best not to intimidate her, but the way that I was feeling, I didn't think that it was working out too well. "She was in that interrogation room for a long time. I've never seen her look so emotional. I can't protect her if I don't know what's coming, Addie."

"Will you?" She sighed. "Will you protect her? Or is she just a new toy to pass the time with?"

"What do you think?" I asked. "I've waited a long time for a chance with her, Adds. I'm not planning on going anywhere."

She nodded before she turned around and hoisted herself up on the worktop behind her. "It's not pretty, Alex. But if you want to know..." She looked down at her lap before she shook her head. "She should have told you this herself."

"How about *you* tell me?" I asked her. "And stop beating around the bush."

She stared at me for several moments before breaking the silence and with it, my heart. "Charlie was pregnant." She pressed her lips together. "It was about a month before she and David broke up. She had taken a test and was planning on telling him but she..." She cleared her throat. "She fell down the stairs. She was okay but she took herself to the hospital as she was bleeding." She pointed to her crotch area, identifying what she meant. "She had lost the baby."

Fucking hell.

"Did she ever tell David?" James asked from the other side of the kitchen.

"No." She shook her head. "She said there was no point as he wouldn't understand. She went to the offices one night a couple of weeks later and found him screwing his receptionist on the desk. She ended it that night."

"Poor Charlie," James whispered.

"She threw herself into her technical job at the call centre and never mentioned it again. And recently, she's seemed happy."

"What do you mean, 'seemed'?" I asked hesitantly.

"She started going out with you and I saw my old Charlie again." She smiled at me. "You made her take a leap on her dream." She jumped down and walked past me. "I'm going to go and see her."

I nodded, letting her go before I turned to face James, who was looking as stunned as I was.

"He's a dead man," I threatened.

CHAPTER
Fourteen

Charlie

Lying in bed the following morning, I groaned at the light coming in through my window. Before I could open my eyes, an arm slid around my waist and I felt warmth cuddle into my back. The scent was too floral to be Alex. Only one person in my life smelled of rosebuds.

"Did you climb into the wrong bed last night?" I teased.

She giggled before leaning over and kissing my cheek. "You know you want me."

I laughed before turning over to face her. "Busted," I mocked. I cuddled my head into the pillow before turning my gaze back to hers. "So, how bad is it out there?" I nodded my head to the closed bedroom door.

"Do I need to go into hiding?" I was only half-joking. Although, I wouldn't have been surprised to find an empty apartment. It was more hassle being with me than it was worth.

I kind of expected her to joke back, but when she only stared at me looking guilty, I knew that it was about more than what happened yesterday.

"I told him about David," she whispered.

I tensed. "What about David?" I asked. I don't know why I was bothering to ask. There was only one thing she could have told Alex about David and it was the one thing I hadn't told him. How did you tell the guy that you were currently with that you almost had a baby with the guy that screwed you over? Literally.

"I told him about the baby, Charlie," she answered, needlessly filling in the blank.

"Addie!" I stared at her, feeling somewhat relieved but also hurt—hurt that she'd abused my trust but also thankful that now I wouldn't have to tell him without becoming an emotional wreck.

"I'm sorry, Charlie! It's just James came to the shop to get me and he looked panicked." She reached up and tucked a loose curl behind my ear. "Alex… He looked so worried. I've never seen him look like that before."

"How did he take it?" I asked. "Was he… Did he get angry?"

"He didn't smash the place up if that's what you're asking. He took it okay from what I saw. After that, I left him and James in the kitchen, and I've been in here with you ever since. Do you want me to go and check if he's still here?"

"No." I shook my head. "He's probably gone home. I'll call him later."

"Okay. Well, I'm going to go and take a shower." She rubbed my arm comfortingly before she left me alone.

I turned over on to my back and stared at the ceiling as I let my thoughts run loose. I still couldn't get over what had happened yesterday at the police station. I think if I hadn't been there, they would have arrested Alex.

I swung my legs out of bed and grabbed my cardigan before tugging it on. It was cream, woollen and had a chunky feel to it. My mum had a knitting hobby, and she was always knitting baby hats for the local hospitals. Whenever I wore this, I always felt like it was a big hug from her. I hadn't called her all week, which made me feel awful. Maybe a visit home to Wales for a few days was to be planned.

I pulled the door open, needing a cup of coffee to knock some life into me. I froze when I saw Alex standing in between the lounge and the kitchen.

"Hi." I was surprised he was still here. I walked through the lounge, hating how hesitant I was to approach him. I had become so comfortable being around him, but now, after yesterday, for the first time, I was unsure about us—unsure how he was after yesterday's big revelation.

"How are you feeling?" he asked. He took a step back as I approached him before he followed me into the kitchen.

"I'm okay." I wrapped the cardigan around me more. "Would you like a coffee?" I asked.

"No, thanks. I should be going, actually."

"I'm sorry," I whispered. "I know how busy you are."

"It's not that." He shook his head and looked past me, staring at the vase of daisies. "I just think maybe you—or we, I guess—need a bit of time."

I hated that my eyes filled at his words. If there was ever a break-up pitch, that was one. The events of yesterday had pushed him too far past what he was comfortable with. It was clear that I was maybe too much drama for the worth of it.

"I see," I choked out. "I'm sorry about yesterday. If this is about what Addie said, I was going to tell you." I was rambling at him now and I know that I must have looked pathetic.

"I don't think you were." He sounded so cold. "I thought that we were honest with each other. I thought…" He chuckled and it sounded so mocking. "I poured my heart out to you. What I told you… I showed the worst part of myself to you, and I thought…" He stared at me for a moment before he spoke again. "I just thought that you trusted me more than that, but I guess that I was wrong." He turned away and began walking out the door. "I was so fucking wrong."

I tensed, expecting him to slam the door when he left but he didn't. Instead, all that followed was silence and dread. I returned to my bedroom and climbed back into bed. Tugging the blankets over my head, I pushed my face into my pillow. Tears fell and little pieces of my heart broke.

Alex was a better man than David would ever be, and I knew that after yesterday—after him finding out what I had kept from him—I would never have another chance. He had walked out of my life, and I didn't think he was ever going to come back.

When someone asks for time and space, it's just a polite way of them trying to get you to go away.

A few hours passed, and I was still hiding in my bed. I was thankful that Addie was getting the message that I didn't want to be bothered. She could sometimes be classed as a blonde ditz, but she had a heart of gold beneath her tough exterior. If she poked her nose in to your business, it was only ever because she wanted to help.

Just as I thought that, my door was kicked open, and

Addie filled up the doorway. She had her hands on her hips and a pissed off expression on her face. "We are still moping then, are we?" She took a few steps into the room before coming to a stop. She cocked her hip to the side and stared down at me. "Do you know how pathetic you're looking right now?"

"Go away." I grabbed the blanket and tugged it over my head, attempting to block her and the intruding light out.

"None of that." She grabbed the blanket and ripped it away before she threw it towards the bottom of the bed, making sure it was out of my grasp. "You need to get out of bed," she ordered.

"Why?" I complained.

"Because, you idiot, you let that guy walk out of here and you didn't even try and stop him. You just stood there and took it." She flopped down next to me on the bed. "I thought you were tougher than that."

"You heard us?" I asked.

"I might have had my ear pressed up against the bathroom door." She rolled her eyes at herself before she continued. "He's hurt, Charlie."

"I did that," I whispered. "I hurt him."

"You did," she said matter-of-factly. "But I think this morning hurt him more."

"What do you mean?" I asked. I was confused. "I didn't do anything this morning."

"Sweetie." She rubbed my pyjama-clad leg before

continuing. "He asked you for space and you agreed." She raised her eyebrows at me. "You covered something up, he found out about it and you just let him go."

"What was I supposed to do?" I asked. "I'm not you, Addie. I'm not as confident in myself as you are. You know what you want and you go after it. I…"

"*You* let him walk out." She tapped my leg before she walked out, leaving me alone. The sound of the apartment door closing soon followed.

I lay in bed for a few moments, silently cursing Addie's name before I swung my legs over the side and headed to the bathroom. As much as I might have hated her directness, I couldn't lie and say that she was wrong. She was right, and that was the part that sucked. I'd just stood there and taken what he'd had to say without complaint, and I hated it. Hated it because that is exactly how I would have acted with David. I'd let him walk all over me like a doormat, and I wasn't prepared to do it again.

Alex was not like David. He was better. He was a good man who had been honest with me and it seemed like it was time for me to start doing the same.

*a*fter taking a shower, I got myself ready—foundation and mascara—and left the apartment. Walking down the block, I probably looked like a crazy person, giving myself a pep talk.

Hearing a whistle, I looked up and saw James standing outside the bar.

"Hi." I waved before crossing the street.

"You seemed kind of out of it there." He grinned at me. "You okay?"

"Not really." I shook my head. "Is Alex in?" I hedged.

"Yeah." He took a drag of his cigarette, inhaling before blowing the smoke away from us. "A little warning. He's not in the best mood."

"I figured." I smoothed my grey, knee-length skirt down before holding my hands out to the side. "How do I look?" I had paired it with a white top—kind of tight for my liking—and my brown jacket.

"Like a million bucks." He gave me a cheeky wink before he nodded his head to the door. "I'd wish you luck but I don't think you'll need it."

"I don't know," I said, disagreeing. "I think I messed it up this morning."

"Just be honest." He slid his hands into his pockets. "If you like, I'll walk in with you."

I nodded, giving him a small smile and followed him through the door.

"James, I need you to go back to the——" Alex stopped talking when he saw me, looking a little surprised.

"Can we talk?" I asked, fidgeting with the strap of my handbag.

He nodded his head. "Sure." Placing the glass down on the bar, he gestured towards his office. "We can talk in here. James, watch the bar." He led the way and waved his hand to the two chairs opposite the desk before closing the door. "Take a seat." Walking around his desk, he sat facing me before he spoke again. "What can I do for you?"

He sounded polite but I could tell that he was tense.

"Nothing." I shook my head, at a loss about what to say next. "I, uh... I'm sorry—again—for yesterday. I should have told you and I—"

"But you didn't," he said, interrupting me. "After the other night, when I told you about my past, I thought that we understood each other."

"I know." I looked down at his desk, hating the way that he was staring at me. I had never seen him look at me so coldly before.

"I understand it was personal for you, and I get that it wasn't exactly an easy topic that you could just bring up but... Fuck, Charlie. What I told you was pretty fucking personal for me, too." He combed his fingers through his hair, appearing agitated. "I just thought that you trusted me."

"I do." I looked up at him. "I do trust you, Alex. I just know that this isn't forever."

His eyes widened in surprise at me, and I knew that my words had shocked him.

"I know that you're not a relationship guy, Alex. I don't know what we are." I bit my lip, hating that we were having this conversation like this. "It's hard for me to give myself over to someone who I know this is a temporary thing for. And now it sounds like I'm asking you to commit to me, which I'm not. It's just…"

"Charlie." He stood and came around his desk before taking the seat next to me. He turned to face me and reached for my hands. "I know that you've heard the rumours about me. I know I've been with a lot of girls and I know that doesn't make me the man of the year." He rolled his eyes at himself before he reached across and rubbed his thumb along my cheekbone. "You're the girl for me. I wouldn't have started this with you if I was going to end it in tears."

I smiled at him, trying to ignore the tears that leaked over my eyelids. "I didn't expect you to be so sweet," I whispered.

"Only with you." He took my hand in his before bringing it to his lips and pressing a kiss to the back of it. "Just no more lies or half-truths. Deal?"

"Deal," I whispered.

CHAPTER
Fifteen

Alex

Watching her sitting at my bar, I chuckled when I saw James helping her. They had been sitting there for the last hour making a pros and cons list on dessert suppliers.

It had been a few days since our argument, and after our promise of no more lies or half-truths, she had confessed to me that she had been struggling at the shop since its grand opening. She hadn't expected it to take off as well as it had, and the early mornings and late finishes were going to wear her down. Since then, she had made some calls to a few suppliers and she now had to decide which ones to use.

"So, remind me again," James said. "Why don't you just outsource everything?"

"Because," she said while huffing, "I love baking. It's why I wanted a shop of my own. I love seeing people enjoying my food." She looked up at me, smiling when she saw me watching her. "I still want to make a lot of the products, but for some items, I could outsource."

"Like donuts," he said, filling in the gap.

"Yes. Like donuts, scones, sandwiches… Maybe the bakewells, the products that have icing on. I already outsource for the crisps and bread." She scribbled some numbers down. "The majority of products I'm not willing to outsource."

"Like the caramel bites," I said, interrupting. It earned me a giggle.

"Yes, like the caramel bites. The desserts I supply to your menu wouldn't be as fresh if I outsourced them. The donuts fly off the shelf and my older customers love the scones with their teas."

"Okay, okay, I think I get it." He reached over and pulled the list of items she had marked down with her pen before he grabbed the supplier sheets. "Let's look at this item by item, then."

For someone who lived in the kitchen, James was pretty dense when it came to discussing someone else's love of all things food.

An hour later, they were both sitting there with giddy expressions on their faces.

"You guys all done?" I asked. I placed a glass of red

wine in front of Charlie before stealing a caramel bite off her plate.

She smirked at me before speaking. "I think so." She slid the paper across to me before taking a sip of her drink.

"This looks a little expensive." I raised my eyes at her over the paper. "Can't you find a cheaper supplier?"

"Quality over quantity. Besides…" She reached for the paper and took it off me before folding it up and sliding her paperwork into her bag. "This means I will have more time to spend with some ruggedly, handsome man."

"Sounds good to me." I leaned over the bar, meeting her halfway and stole a kiss from her.

"Also, the shop can cover it and it might leave me with enough revenue to take on another member of staff." She sounded perky, and it made me relieved that she seemed to be looking at this in a positive light.

"Which means you could maybe have some late morning starts." I wiggled my eyebrows at her, loving the blush that spread along her cheeks. "That reminds me. Did you hear back from the police?"

Her face dropped when I mentioned the 'p' word, and I knew it was because she had been trying to put it out of her mind.

"They rang me this morning," she admitted. "They have requested that he keep his distance, which he has agreed to. If he doesn't, they will petition for a restraining order."

"Does that make you feel better?" I asked. Sometimes her face was so easy to read, but right now, she had a poker face.

"A little. I just wish he would move on." She shrugged her shoulders. "Addie thinks he thought I would have gone back to him—that maybe I would have put up with what he did to me?" She ended it as a question.

"Do you think you could have?" I asked. "Do you think if you didn't have Addie to share your problems with, you would have given in?"

She stared up at me for a few moments before responding. "Maybe. I don't know."

I nodded, accepting her answer before I went down the bar to serve some customers.

"*S*ee you tomorrow," James called as he headed toward the exit. "Have fun."

I laughed, knowing full well what he meant. Charlie had disappeared up to my apartment an hour ago, insisting that she was exhausted. She had stayed over a couple of times but tonight felt different. Her staying over tonight was the first time since we had admitted to each other that we were more to each other than just a temporary arrangement.

I quickly locked up, and after setting the alarm and checking all the doors and windows, I turned the electrics off and headed upstairs.

Walking in, I chuckled when I saw little signs of her everywhere: shoes by the door, cardigan on the sofa, a worn copy of Lovebomb by Sienna Grant she'd been reading on the coffee table and a tub of caramel bites on the kitchen worktop with a lipstick kiss on a post-it note.

I grinned when I saw her lying on my bed. The soft rise and fall of her chest told me that she was sleeping. She was in a pink tank top and shorts, taking up most of the bed and lying in a starfish pose.

I took my phone out of my pocket and snapped a picture of her before toeing off my shoes and changing into a pair of pyjama bottoms. Normally it'd just be underwear for me, but lately, I had a feeling she compared herself to my past sexual adventures. I wanted her to feel that this was more than just a string of one-night stands. We had more than that.

They had fuck all on my girl. Charlie was sexy without even trying to be.

Gently taking hold of her wrists, I placed them around my neck before sliding my arms beneath her and lifting her up into my arms. Moving the blanket back, I placed her under it before climbing in beside her.

I reached over and turned the lamp off, sliding my arm around her waist and cuddled closer to her, spooning her gorgeous body. I closed my eyes, the tension beginning to leave my body when her voice spoke out.

"Good night, Alex."

I reached down and kissed her shoulder before laying my head back on the pillow. "Good night, darling."

---

*W*aking up the following morning, I smiled when I felt movement next to me. I had expected her to have left by now and be at the shop, but as I felt her warmth against my side, I was happy to be wrong.

"Good morning," she whispered. She leaned up on her elbows and kissed me.

"It definitely is." I chuckled against her lips, loving how she felt against my side. "I could get used to this."

She giggled, resting her head against my shoulder. She trailed her fingers across my stomach, making patterns with her fingertips.

"What are you doing?" I asked.

"Touching you." She lowered her head and kissed my shoulder. "Does it feel good? My touch?"

I groaned. "It does." I could feel myself hardening, and I know that she could see it as well.

She moved her hand further down before sliding her fingers beneath the waistband of my pyjamas.

"Charlie!" I grabbed her hand, halting her movements.

"Let me touch you," she whispered. "Make you feel good." She dipped her hand lower and rubbed her fingers along my shaft. "Pull your bottoms down," she whispered in my ear before licking the lobe.

I lifted my hips and yanked my trousers down over my waist, my cock springing free. I shoved the blankets down, groaning when she grasped me tighter in her hand.

"Is this okay?" she asked. She pumped me a couple of times before she licked behind my ear.

"Like this," I whispered. I reached down and placed my hand over hers before bringing her hand up and pumping my cock faster. She tightened her grip, following my direction. "Ah, fuck." I roughly turned her face to mine and thrust my tongue into her mouth.

She slid her palm over the head of my cock before moving back down. On the next pass, she reached down and fondled my balls, making my eyes roll back in my head. I rocked my hips before guiding her hand again.

"I wish I was fucking you right now." I tilted my head back against the pillow, imagining how fuckable she would be riding me.

She giggled before nibbling on my earlobe. "Good things come to those who wait," she teased me.

After a few quick pumps, I tore her hand from my cock and took over, not stopping until I was ejaculating on my stomach. I groaned as the pleasure moved through me before looking at her.

"That was kind of hot," she admitted.

I laughed at her before grabbing my t-shirt off the floor and wiping the mess away. Reaching down, I tucked myself back in my trousers and yanked her down to me.

She shrieked at the action, lying half on top of me.

"You are not helping," I growled. I reached up and grabbed her breasts, rubbing them. She moaned at the action before I felt her rock her hips against me. I grabbed the straps of her vest, moving them down her arms, determined to move this along.

"Stop," she whispered. She pulled away from me, rolled over and climbed out of bed. "I need to get to the shop."

I groaned as I watched her sexy arse in those shorts walking away from me.

"You're just going to leave me here?" I sat up against the pillows, watching my sexy minx tease me.

She slipped her shorts down and removed her strappy top, leaving her in only a pair of sexy, yellow, lacy knickers.

"You're killing me."

She giggled, covering her breasts from my eye with a matching bra. Minutes later, she was pulling her cream top on and wrapping a skirt around her waist. "I might make it up to you." She walked over and bent down, kissing me before pulling back. "If those caramel bites are still there later, I may reward you."

"Fucking minx," I responded. I climbed out of bed and followed her out of the door, staring at her sexy as sin legs as she approached the door. "I'll take you down." I placed my hands on her shoulders as she walked in front of me.

The last few days we had become closer—physically and emotionally—and I was filled with this constant need to always be touching her.

"Dinner tonight?" I asked when we were standing outside. "I can cook for us. At yours, preferably? Fewer interruptions."

"Addie might be there," she replied. "I can ask her and see what her plans are."

"Don't worry about Addie," I replied. "I'll have a word with James and see what's happening."

Her eyes widened in surprise. "James?" She gasped. "Do you think something is going on between them?"

"When Addie told me about"—he pointed at my stomach—"that," he continued. "I watched the way that she spoke to him and she... I don't know. They looked kind of familiar with each other."

"Well, they *are* friends," I interjected. "Maybe that's all there is."

"Maybe." I reached down for another kiss. "I'll see you tonight."

"Okay." She gave me a beaming smile before she turned away and walked next door.

I stood there at the door for a little longer, chuckling when I saw she already had a few customers waiting outside, even though the shop didn't open for another half hour.

Walking inside, I sent a text message to James asking him to keep Addie busy tonight. As I waited for the reply, I thought over what I was going to cook for Charlie. I wanted to make it special as she had been under more than enough stress and drama lately.

My phone beeped, alerting me to a response. That was quick.

Got plans? ;)

Nosey fucker.

I'll ask Scott and a couple of the boys to mind the bar tonight. Have Addie stay at yours.

Stepping behind the bar, I groaned when I saw we were getting low on the fruity gins again. There were a few boxes in the storeroom but they were getting popular with the customers.

Fine. Have a good night. Thought you should know… David was hanging around outside the bar last night

Fucking great.

———————

*a*fter a shower—spent mostly trying not to think about how good Charlie would look up against the tiles—and a change of clothes, I went back downstairs with my tablet and headed to the storeroom and began the stock check.

Several hours passed, and after getting the boys caught up with the night's reservations, I was leaving. "I have my phone on me so if there are any problems, call me." I waved it at them, waiting for a head nod from each of them. "I'm only down the block, so if the place catches fire…" I joked.

I walked down the street, heading for one of the supermarkets, needing to pick up a few items for tonight's meal. I needed it to be perfect. I needed us to have just one night away from all the stresses and dramas—from the craziness that had become our lives lately.

After grabbing the supplies and a bottle of Charlie's favourite palma violet flavoured purple gin, I was at her apartment building, pressing the buzzer and waiting for Addie to answer. The sound of the buzzer interrupted my thoughts before Addie's voice came through the speaker.

"Come on up, Casanova."

I rolled my eyes at the nickname she had dubbed me with and ran up the steps. I chuckled when she already had the door open for me.

"Thanks for tonight, Addie."

"Yeah, yeah." She leaned up and kissed me on the cheek before stepping back and reaching for her jacket. She slid her arms through the sleeves. "So, what're the plans for tonight? I'm guessing tonight is a special night or something."

"Not really." I huffed when I saw her cocking her eyebrow at me. "It's nothing! I just wanted Charlie and me to have a night drama-free. Just her, me and nothing else."

"Aw! Look at you." She grabbed her handbag off the worktop before applying a coat of lipstick. Checking her reflection in the mirror, she did a little twirl, giving herself a once over. "Who would have ever guessed that Mr. Tough Bartender would become so whipped?"

"I'm not whipped." I rolled my eyes at her before walking past her. "Will you be back tonight?" I asked.

"I think I'll pass." She untucked her hair from beneath her jacket. "I'll stay at a friend's."

"Like James?" I mocked. "I think something is going on there."

She made a dismissive noise before she waved at me and walked to the door. "He wishes."

I rolled my eyes at her, laying all the items out, and began planning the meal. I wasn't a fan of cooking, but Addie wasn't wrong when she said I was becoming whipped.

I was man enough to admit it.

Nosey fucker.

I'll ask Scott and a couple of the boys to mind the bar tonight. Have Addie stay at yours.

Stepping behind the bar, I groaned when I saw we were getting low on the fruity gins again. There were a few boxes in the storeroom but they were getting popular with the customers.

Fine. Have a good night. Thought you should know… David was hanging around outside the bar last night

Fucking great.

---

*a*fter a shower—spent mostly trying not to think about how good Charlie would look up against the tiles—and a change of clothes, I went back downstairs with my tablet and headed to the storeroom and began the stock check.

Several hours passed, and after getting the boys caught up with the night's reservations, I was leaving. "I have my phone on me so if there are any problems, call me." I waved it at them, waiting for a head nod from each of them. "I'm only down the block, so if the place catches fire…" I joked.

I walked down the street, heading for one of the supermarkets, needing to pick up a few items for tonight's meal. I needed it to be perfect. I needed us to have just one night away from all the stresses and dramas—from the craziness that had become our lives lately.

After grabbing the supplies and a bottle of Charlie's favourite palma violet flavoured purple gin, I was at her apartment building, pressing the buzzer and waiting for Addie to answer. The sound of the buzzer interrupted my thoughts before Addie's voice came through the speaker.

"Come on up, Casanova."

I rolled my eyes at the nickname she had dubbed me with and ran up the steps. I chuckled when she already had the door open for me.

"Thanks for tonight, Addie."

"Yeah, yeah." She leaned up and kissed me on the cheek before stepping back and reaching for her jacket. She slid her arms through the sleeves. "So, what're the plans for tonight? I'm guessing tonight is a special night or something."

"Not really." I huffed when I saw her cocking her eyebrow at me. "It's nothing! I just wanted Charlie and me to have a night drama-free. Just her, me and nothing else."

"Aw! Look at you." She grabbed her handbag off the worktop before applying a coat of lipstick. Checking her reflection in the mirror, she did a little twirl, giving herself a once over. "Who would have ever guessed that Mr. Tough Bartender would become so whipped?"

"I'm not whipped." I rolled my eyes at her before walking past her. "Will you be back tonight?" I asked.

"I think I'll pass." She untucked her hair from beneath her jacket. "I'll stay at a friend's."

"Like James?" I mocked. "I think something is going on there."

She made a dismissive noise before she waved at me and walked to the door. "He wishes."

I rolled my eyes at her, laying all the items out, and began planning the meal. I wasn't a fan of cooking, but Addie wasn't wrong when she said I was becoming whipped.

I was man enough to admit it.

CHAPTER Sixteen

David

Watching her coming out of Alex's bar, I had never felt so angry. Her hair was rumpled and she had a stupid smile on her face. She thought that she was happy with him but she didn't know. She didn't know how much of a fool she was being.

He was a beast. He didn't deserve an angel like her. I knew that I didn't either anymore. I had fucked up, and I knew that there was nothing that I could do to take it back. I'd screwed another woman behind her back, and she had every right toss me to the kerb. However, if she thought that I was going to accept being replaced by that monster, she was so fucking wrong.

Walking into The Dark Room—not a lot of thought put into the title of that club—I walked up to the bar and ordered a scotch on the rocks. I had always been a drinker, but since Charlie had quit her job and opened her little café shop, it had gotten worse.

When we'd broken up, I had been a cocky prick. I thought she'd be back to me in a week, but then her interfering supposed best friend stuck her nose in and she never came back. She collected her stuff, cut contact and changed her telephone numbers. Fuck, even her email address was closed down.

I had begun going to her place of work. It was the only place that I knew I would see her. First, it had started as just once a week—sitting outside on my lunch break having a sandwich—but then it had slowly morphed into a few times a week and before I knew it, it had progressed to following her home and hanging around outside her apartment complex.

I looked at my reflection in the mirror behind the bar, disgusted with myself. I'd always been a well-respected businessman, and I had now been reduced to an idiot who had to be warned by the police to stay away.

Before I could get sucked back down memory lane, a hand clamped down on my shoulder from behind.

"Mr. Smith," a deep, male voice sounded from behind me. "The boss would like to see you."

I nodded, downing my glass and turned around,

slipping off my stool and followed the big man to the back of the club. I looked around, noticing that the club was full of bikers and big guys that appeared a little thuggish. I didn't belong here with these low-lives and it was pathetic that this was what I had been reduced to: sneaking around in dark clubs, meeting with assholes that I would usually cross over the street to avoid.

We walked through a closed door that was marked 'STAFF ONLY'. It had a keypad on the side by the frame, and after the big guy in the suit typed in a pin code, he pushed the door open and we walked down a corridor. It was lined with doors on each side but we didn't stop until we got to the one at the end. I waited for a sign to indicate what sort of room it was we were walking into but there wasn't any.

"Come on in," another male voice said.

Big guy stood to the side and indicated for me to take a chair in front of the desk. He walked away when I took a seat and shut the door loudly behind him.

"So, Mr. Smith. What can I do for you?"

He was a young man, dressed in a dark suit with a matching shirt and tie. Just like Johnny Cash, he looked like he was going to a funeral. He had dark hair and a bit of stubble on his face.

"I want some information," I said, blunt and straight to the point. "I have been told that you are a friend of Alex Winters."

The young man smirked at me before leaning

forwards and placing his arms on the desk. "Alex Winters." He rubbed his fingers across his chin. "I haven't heard that name in a while. Why do you want to know about Alex Winters? He owe you money?"

"No." I shook my head. "We have a mutual friend in common and I… I know that he's a bad guy. I was told you knew him."

He stared at me coldly before answering. "I know him. He's got your girl, right? Charlotte Chase?"

My blood ran cold. I didn't like that he knew her name, and judging by the glint in his eye, I assumed that he knew a lot of other things about her that he shouldn't really fucking know.

"I make it my business to keep up to date on all my clients, Mr. Smith."

"Is that what he is?" I asked. "A client?"

"A friend." He shrugged his shoulders. "We served time together."

"Prison?" I asked, surprised. "What did he do?"

"I don't think that's any of your business." He glared at me, resting his chin in his hand. "Now, why don't you tell me the real reason you came here?"

I stared at him, agitated. I knew this arsehole had the answer I needed. I knew he could give me the key to demolishing the little world that Charlie had created with Alex, and I really didn't want to leave here without it.

"I need a gun," I answered. "I know I can get one here."

"And what makes you think that?" he asked. He had a terrific poker face.

"Because I'm not stupid!" I snapped. "I need to protect myself, and I can't rely on the police to do fuck all for me. Plus, I can pay you."

He nodded his head before standing up and walking past me. "Come with me." I followed him back through the door and down the corridor before we stopped halfway and he led me in through another door.

I took a step back in surprise, shocked as fuck at what I was seeing. The room was full of glass display cabinets with all sorts of weaponry on show. He walked over to a cabinet, pulling a small black case out. He opened it and moved it closer to me. Inside was a black handgun.

Before I could reach for it, he pulled it away from me, shaking his head at the man who was standing behind me. I assumed he was telling him to put his gun away: a place like that didn't get this stocked without some security.

"We're not a charity here, Mr. Smith. Payment upfront."

I nodded my head, producing a brown envelope from inside my suit pocket with five grand of cash.

"Do I need to count it?" he mocked. "By the way,

Mr. Smith, how did you come to know of my little business?"

I rolled my eyes at him. The fucker was trying to act all business-like and professional when he was just a fucking criminal. "We have a mutual friend." I stared at him. "I know your man, William, and he said that you were trustworthy and wouldn't ask too many questions."

He smirked at me. "Fair enough."

I shook my head and grabbed the box with the gun and bullets before marching towards the door.

"A word of advice, Mr. Smith," he called after me, making me stop at the door. "I wouldn't go waving that around near our dear friend, Alex."

"Why not?" I asked.

Who the fuck did he think he was talking to?! I could handle myself.

"Because he won't hesitate to use that gun on you."

I stared at him, shocked at the threat. I nodded my head slowly and continued my walk out of the door. I took his advice for what it was. It was a warning—a warning to not turn my back on Alex and to get Charlie out.

CHAPTER
Seventeen

Charlie

Walking, I dumped my bag by the door and walked quietly around the corner. Leaning against the wall, I smiled as I watched him standing at the stove. He was mixing what looked like a sauce and had a pot of boiling pasta. It looked like he was making me my favourite meal: spaghetti and meatballs.

I walked further into the room, sliding my arms around his waist.

"Hey." He placed his hand over mine where it was resting on his stomach. "How was the café?"

I groaned, shuffling backward and hopped up on the worktop behind me. "It was a long day." I swung my legs from side to side, giggling when he stared over his shoulder at my legs peeking out from beneath my skirt. I toed my ballet flats off, letting them drop to the floor. "Am I distracting you?"

He turned the sauce down before he turned to me, not stopping until he was standing between my parted legs.

"You know you are." He grabbed my thighs and lifted them against his hips, tugging my arse to the edge of the worktop. "You torment me."

I moaned when I felt his lips against my neck.

"Where's Addie?" I asked.

He pulled back, looking down at me with his eyebrows raised. "I can't be doing this right if you're thinking about Addie."

I laughed before placing my hand on his chest and pushed him back a little. "I'm going to go and wash up, if that's okay."

"Sure." He went back to the stove. "I'd offer my assistance, but I think if I did that, you'd be in there a lot longer."

"Then I guess you had better stay there and cook my food," I called over my shoulder as I left the kitchen.

"You're sexy when you boss me around," he said before grating the cheese at the worktop.

I quickly stripped in my room and wrapped a towel around myself and escaped to the bathroom. Climbing into the shower, I sighed as I felt the hot warmth from the spray soothe the tense muscles in my shoulders.

I had underestimated how physically draining it would be working at the café. I had naively once imagined that if I had the dream job and found the dream guy that everything else would fall into place. I slowly realised that the dream job didn't exist and neither did the dream guy.

The guy in my kitchen though... I think he was as close as I was going to get.

I quickly rinsed my hair and climbed from the shower cubicle. Wrapping a towel around my body, I patted myself dry before cursing at not bringing clothes in with me. Reaching for the door handle, I swung the door open and froze when I saw Alex standing at the door, checking the locks.

As much as he tried to hide his paranoia, I was sure he was still worried the door wasn't fully secure, even though he had been the one to fit new locks. I didn't think the apartment could get any safer.

He turned around, finding me behind him. He froze when he saw me, his eyes immediately going down to my chest. Water droplets dripped from my face before trailing down my chest where they disappeared beneath the towel that was wrapped snugly around my chest. His eyes followed the movement before he reached for me. He grasped my hips and pulled me towards him. He leaned up and pressed his pointer finger against my collar bone gently before trailing it down and drawing random patterns over my upper chest.

I loved it when he touched me. When he was near me, he made me feel things that I had never once felt with David. Alex made me come alive.

His throat bobbed before he took a step back. "You had better go in your bedroom," he gritted out. "Otherwise you're not going to have dinner." He walked past me, going back to the kitchen before stopping. "Ten minutes?"

"No problem." I escaped to my bedroom, drying myself off and changing into a new pair of pyjamas, a t-shirt and three-quarter length bottoms. I took a deep breath, trying to stop the way my thoughts were going. Right now, I just wanted to pull him in here with me and not come out till tomorrow. Shaking my head, I quickly dried my hair. I checked my reflection, sliding a comb through it and plaiting it, pinning it back out of my face before I joined him back in the kitchen.

"It smells very yummy in here."

"Take a seat at the table." He pointed his head to my small, round kitchen table.

I did as he asked, smiling when he placed a plate of meatballs in front of me with a heaping mound of spaghetti bolognaise in tomato sauce.

"How did you know this was my favourite meal?" I asked.

He winked at me as he took a seat next to me. "I do not disclose my sources." He forked some spaghetti into his mouth before standing back up and going to the fridge.

"Do you want a wine or beer?" he asked.

"Surprise me." I speared a piece of meatball before soaking it in some of the sauce and bringing it to my mouth.

He re-joined me, placing a couple of bottles of Budweiser on the table. We ate our meals in silence for a few moments before he reached over and placed his hand on mine. He gave it a gentle squeeze before he spoke.

"This is nice."

"It is." I moved my hand over his, smiling at him when he lifted it and pressed a kiss to the back of it. "It's nice that we can do this after everything that's happened lately."

"Come on!" he mocked. "I thought our trip to the police station was pretty memorable."

I rolled my eyes at his teasing, secretly thankful that it appeared he was no longer angry or hurt about what had happened that day. I couldn't deny that it hadn't gone without its fallout but it appeared that we had both come through it.

"I still can't believe David tried to have you arrested." I was mortified that it had happened. "I mean, what if he had been successful?"

"Then I would have gone back to a cell." He grinned at me.

"That's not funny, Alex." I pushed my plate away a little before standing and walking away. Taking a seat on the sofa, I sighed when I thought back to my time with David. I wished that I had seen how much of a monster he was before all of this.

Alex walked into the lounge after a few moments, holding both of our drinks. He handed my bottle to me and took a seat beside me, leaving a space in between us. He took a swig of his bottle before he patted his lap.

I lifted my legs and slid my feet into his lap, moaning when he began massaging the underside of my feet before focusing on my heels.

"That feel good?" he rasped.

"So good." I took a sip of my drink before relaxing back further. "I didn't realise how exhausting baking all day could be."

"I think you underestimated it all." He looked over at me, frowning. "I think you're overdoing it."

I stared at him for a few moments, feeling oddly touched when I realised what I could see reflected back at me in his irises: worry, concern... I didn't think that I had ever had either from David. "Thank you," I whispered. "Thank you for thinking of me." I twisted my ankle and trailed my toes over his wrist. "I'm slowly realising that you do that a lot."

He shook his head before his shoulders dropped. For a moment, he looked disappointed. "You shouldn't have to thank someone for thinking of you." He turned his head back to me. "It makes me angry: it's obvious that David never did. Think of you, that is."

"He did," I said, disagreeing. "He just thought of himself more."

"He's a fool." He reached his hand out for mine before he pulled me up and yanked me closer to him. He rearranged me, placing me across his lap. "To not see what he had. To not want to be like this with you whenever he could." His eyes trailed down to my neck before he leaned his head back against the cushion and looked back up into my eyes. "I can never seem to stop touching you." He trailed his hands beneath my t-shirt, whispering his fingers against my skin.

"You're sounding very sweet, Alex. I always took you as a bad boy. I had no idea that we could be like this." I scraped my fingers through his soft hair, running my nails along his scalp. I expected a witty comeback, but he just stared up at me. When he looked at me like this, I always felt like his chocolate brown orbs saw more in me than I was willing to share—more than I had allowed anyone else to see. "What?" I asked. "What are you staring at?"

"You." He reached up and took my face in his hands, tangling his fingers into the hair behind my ears. "Just you." He slowly pulled my face down to his and softly nibbled my bottom lip, sucking it into his mouth. He pulled my forehead down to rest against his before he closed his eyes.

"You're frightening me," I whispered.

He chuckled. "Then what I am about to say to you is going to terrify you."

"I can handle it." I strengthened my voice, trying to demonstrate that I could. "It won't change anything between us."

"If you say so." He leaned back up and kissed me. This time he thrust his tongue in between my parted lips, stealing my breath from me. After a moment, he pulled back before whispering, "I think I'm falling for you."

I stared down at him in surprise before I pulled back, disentangling myself from his grasp. "Uh..." I shuffled back into my seat, tightening my grip on the bottle. "Okay. We can talk about that."

He chuckled before he turned to face me. "I have freaked you out." He picked his bottle up from where it was standing at his feet. He took a swig and continued. "Trust me. I am just as surprised as you are."

"Have you ever..." I scratched my eyebrow, collecting my thoughts. "Have you ever felt this way about anyone else?"

"No." He reached over and took my hand, rubbing his thumb across my knuckles. "I'm sorry. I didn't mean to surprise you this much."

"You didn't." The lie came so easily from my lips that I wanted to slap myself. "You did." I rolled my eyes at myself. "It's just a little fast."

He flattened his lips before he breathed out a sigh. "I understand that." He stood up, walking over to the window and gazed out on to the street below. He dropped his hands to his sides before he clenched his right hand into a fist a few times and dropped it back to his side. "I'm sorry that you don't feel the same."

Now I felt like a bitch. He had just opened his heart a little more to me and he had probably felt like me removing myself from his hold as throwing it back in his face a little.

"I didn't say that," I reasoned. "I just said it was a little fast."

"Fast." He stared out into the night before he straightened his posture. "Do you know how long I have wanted you? Every time that I saw you with that piece of shit, I wanted to smash my fist into his face. I have only ever felt that sort of loss of control once, and it was a time that the course of my life had changed." He turned around and stared at me, unapologetic. "When I saw you walk into my bar for the first time, it happened again."

"We were friends," I whispered.

"No." He put his hands into his pockets. "I was *your* friend. You—" He turned back to the window, hiding his eyes from mine. "You were the girl that I always wanted and found that I could never have—that I would never be worthy of."

CHAPTER
Eighteen

Alex

I was a fucking jackass.

Why the fuck did I decide to tell her how I was feeling after all of the bullshit that she had recently gone through?!

She was right. It *was* too fast. Well, for her it was.

When she had been with David, I hadn't been blind. I'd seen the way that she looked at him. When they were together, it had been pretty safe to estimate that she'd felt for him what I thought I was feeling for her.

"We were friends," she whispered shakily. She sounded like she was trying to convince herself that that's what we were.

"No," I disagreed before putting my hands in my pockets. "I was *your* friend. You—" I sighed before

turning back to the window, unable to look at her.
"You were the girl that I'd always wanted and found
that I could never have—that I would never be
worthy of."

Ever.

I stared down at the street, focusing on the taxi that
was parked at the kerb. He was waiting for a fare and
that's when I realised we had that in common.

We were both waiting.

I decided that I would always be waiting for her.
After what she had been through with David—and was
still going through with him—it was unfair for me to
stand here and expect her to feel for me in the same
way. She was the first woman who I could picture an
actual future with. Just because I was finally ready to
settle down, it didn't mean that she was.

"I should go." I turned around, but before I could
attempt to move past her, she shot up and put herself in
my path, blocking my way to the door.

"Don't go." She placed her hands on my chest,
stopping me. "Don't leave. I'm sorry. You just surprised
me."

"I shouldn't have said anything." I wrapped my arm
around her shoulders before pulling her against me. "I
mean, you *did* say you thought that we would be a
temporary thing, didn't you?"

She fisted my t-shirt in her hands and cuddled her
head into the centre of my chest.

A few moments of silence passed before she eventually spoke up.

"I don't want us to be temporary," she muttered. She lifted her head and gazed up at me. "I think I had just convinced myself that we would be."

"Why?" I asked, needing to know.

"David hurt me, Alex," she whispered. Her eyes glistened up at me. "I don't know how I would handle it if you did that to me."

"I promise not to cheat with a member of my staff," I joked, trying to lighten the mood.

She giggled, leading me back to the sofa. She took the middle seat and cuddled against my side before tugging my arm around her shoulders.

"I think you and Scott would make a cute couple." She grinned at my look of disgust.

"I prefer redheads," I teased before pulling her lips up to mine.

We spent the rest of the evening on the sofa before we finally called it a night and went to the bedroom. After checking the locks, I pulled my t-shirt up and over my head and discarded my jeans on the floor. I turned the light off and climbed into bed, pulling Charlie against me. I tangled my legs with hers and wrapped my arm around her, entwining our fingers. We fell asleep in each other's arms, and as I lay there, holding her, that was the moment that I made a promise to myself.

I would wait for her. However long it took. She was worth waiting for.

———

The next day, we walked to her shop, sharing a coffee and donut before I made my way next door to the bar. I had a delivery today and I needed to be there to check it. The last time we'd had one from this supplier, I'd had a suspicion that we hadn't received everything. I had left James in charge last time and he was terrible at paperwork. He just ticked everything off without checking usually, so I had no proof of it.

"How did it go?" James asked from behind the bar. "Good night?"

I glared at him as I walked past him, heading for the stairs to my apartment. A shower was needed.

"That good, huh?" he called after me. He was like the male version of Addie. No wonder they both spent so much time together. They were both gossip queens.

I jogged up the stairs, stripping as soon as I got through the door. Walking into the bathroom, I tossed my dirty clothes aside and hopped in the shower, soaping myself up. It was the quickest shower in history. I had suppliers coming and a clueless brother when it came to audit checks.

After wrapping a towel around my waist, I walked

through my lounge, needing a drink. I knew I had water in the fridge, and opening the door, I saw a clear plastic bottle standing at the back. I quickly grabbed it and unscrewed it, taking a large gulp from it.

Before I could take another swig, a sound from behind had me freezing. I reached forwards, grasping the handle of a black knife that was propped up in the knife block sitting on top of the worktop.

"Now, now," a voice mocked from behind me. "I thought we were past the violence stage of our friendship."

I didn't need to look to confirm what I knew. It was a voice that I'd never wanted to hear again for as long as I lived. Fate, however, had other plans. "I didn't think I'd see you again," I said, replacing the knife in its slot. I turned around, attempting to relax my shoulders and let the tension go. "What brings you here?" I may have appeared laidback but I was the farthest fucking thing from it. This man was a stone-cold killer, and I knew to be careful around a man like this.

Anton Giovanni.

I had spent five years at his side in prison. I had been a sinner when I went to prison, but this man had turned me into a monster—a monster that I wasn't willing to unleash into the world again.

"I'd like us to talk." He cocked his head behind him to the lounge. "Go and put some clothes on." He turned away and walked into the lounge.

I glared at his back before I did as he directed and walked to my room. I quickly grabbed a t-shirt and jeans before pulling on a pair of socks. I wasn't in the fucking mood for this bullshit today. I had said goodbye to this part of my life, and there was no fucking way I was going to let it back in now.

"What do you want?" I asked. I took a seat in the chair opposite him.

He smirked at me and I knew he was thinking about knocking me out. Anton was the perfect example of everything that was wrong and cruel in this world: hitman, killer, gun dealer, drug cartel... He was a vicious animal.

"Who's the girl?" he asked. His eyes flicked behind me, no doubt looking for signs of her.

"What girl?" I asked back immediately.

"I don't like liars," he threatened. "You know that."

"Why are you here?" I asked.

He stared at me for a few moments before he looked at the door. "Bring him in!" he called loudly.

Seconds later, the door to my apartment opened and in walked two guards of his security. They dragged my brother in with them and threw him to the floor.

"What the fuck is this?" I shouted, waving my hand to James. "I thought we were cool."

"We are." He nodded his head at me. "I haven't forgotten what I did for you and I know you haven't, either." He smiled at me coldly.

"I had a visitor the other day, Alexander." His eyes flicked to James still kneeling on the floor before coming back to me. "David. Smith." He pronounced each of his names slowly before continuing. "I believe you all know each other?"

"I, uh..."

"It's okay." He raised his hand dismissively. "You don't need to explain anything."

"He didn't get your name from me," I quickly interjected. "He and I aren't exactly the best of friends."

"So, how do you think he got my name?" he asked. He was oozing confidence, and it made me think that he already knew the answer.

"I don't know." That fucking bastard was determined to make my life a living hell. "He didn't get it from me." I maintained eye contact with him to show that I wasn't lying. "I swear."

"I believe you." He nodded his head before he walked past me and walked to the door.

He fucking knew.

"What did he have off you?" I asked. I needed to know what type of shit-storm was coming my way.

He slowly turned to face me, taking his sweet time in confessing. Before I could lose my patience, he spoke, shattering the peace that I thought I had finally found. "He bought a gun." He gave me a two-fingered salute and turned back to the door. "Watch your back, Alex."

I watched him walk out the door before turning to James. "We need to talk," I said.

He nodded his head, getting up and taking the seat that Anton had vacated.

I sighed before I started pacing to the window and back. "I don't know where to start."

"Just say what he did for you," he said bluntly. "And who the fuck *is* that guy? He looks like a stand-in for a bad mafia movie."

I chuckled. His description wasn't too far off the mark. "Anton was my cellmate," I shakily admitted. "He was pretty much the big guy in prison. Top dog if you like."

"He looked out for you?" James asked, trying to fill in the blanks.

"Yeah." I took a seat back in the chair opposite him, hating the truth that I was forced to share. "It wasn't a pretty place, James. I did things in that hellhole that I'm not proud of."

"Like what?" he asked, pushing further. "You never talk about your time in prison."

"Because I hated it there. I counted down every day to my release, bro." I was getting agitated now. "I worked for Anton in prison: collected debts for him, organised beat downs, helped pass drugs from cell to cell, took part in fights for him..." I shrugged my shoulders. "It helped to keep my nose clean and it made sure I got out on time."

"I'm guessing something else happened."

"Yeah." I tightened my hands into fists before I continued. "A few weeks before my release, a guard found drugs on me."

"Fuck," he gasped.

"Anton took the fall for me. A couple of years got added on to his sentence and I got to leave the big house when my time was done." I ground my teeth. "Anton got me out of prison."

"So, he's a decent guy, then?" James asked. He was grasping for straws, trying to convince himself that we were okay.

"No. He's not." I rubbed my hands together, feeling anxious. "I always knew I would owe him one day. It was a debt, and now it looks like it's time to pay the price."

"Wait, what happened to the guard? I mean, he was a witness to you having the drugs, right?"

I stared at him. "Anton's a powerful man. Even back then he was." I blew out a deep breath. "The guard was involved in a hit and run accident."

"Fuck, man." He looked at me with sympathy and I fucking hated it. "What do you think he's going to ask for?" James asked.

I shook my head. "I doubt he'll ask for anything yet. I'm pretty sure we will see him again though."

CHAPTER
Nineteen

Charlie

It had been a few days since I had last seen Alex. We had both been so busy with our own businesses that the relationship had been forced to take a back seat. We had spoken on the phone and had been sending messages back and forth but that was it. I had thought more than once about sneaking over to his place one evening, but I had often crashed and fallen asleep on the sofa, waking up to a dark apartment.

I had put orders in to suppliers for some baked goods, and my workload had lessened a little since their first delivery. I was happy about that, and the customers seemed to really enjoy them so it was a win-win situation.

I'd woken up early, excited for the day ahead. I had

stayed late last night, making extra goods for today and storing them in the fridge in the kitchen to keep them fresh. Addie was looking after the shop today, which meant that I had the whole day to hopefully spend with Alex.

I grabbed my bag and left the apartment and walked down to where Alex's bar was at the end of the block. I waved to a few customers before I grabbed the door handle, frowning when it wouldn't budge. I guessed they hadn't opened up yet.

Looking around the corner, I noticed James's car was parked outside the gate to the side door, so I followed the path, relieved when I found it was unlocked. I gently closed it before following the corridor behind the bar and slowly walked up the steps to Alex's apartment.

I pulled the caramel bites out of my bag that I had made especially for him. I raised my hand to knock but noticed that the door was ajar. Frowning, I wondered what was going on when I heard James's and Alex's voices coming from inside.

"When are you going to tell her?" James asked. He had a bit of a snappy tone to his voice. "She needs to know what's going on. You can't keep avoiding her."

"I'm not avoiding her!" Alex fired back at him. "I just need to get Anton the fuck away from here before she…"

I couldn't stand there any longer. David had lied to

me so many times, and now here Alex was basically doing the same thing. He was supposed to be different from him and now... Now I was being made to feel as though I wasn't good enough to share in his problems.

"Before she what?" I asked. I walked inside, reaching back and shutting the door loudly.

Both of their heads turned sharply to where I was standing.

"Well?" I asked. I put his sweet treats back in my bag before placing it down against the wall. "It sounded like you were—what's the word I'm looking for?" I asked sarcastically. "Oh, yeah." I placed my hand on my hips before continuing. "Avoiding me."

"I'm not avoiding you," Alex said, standing up and turning to face me.

"No!" I said, pointing my finger at him. "Avoiding would be something, but what I just walked in on..." I glared at him. "Right now, you're doing more than avoiding me. You're lying to me!" My voice broke at my outburst, and I fucking hated that I couldn't be strong about this without my stupid emotions getting in the way.

"I think I should go," James interjected before trying to walk past me.

"No!" I shouted at him. "No. I want you to stay and I want you both to tell me what the *hell* is going on. Right now!"

James widened his eyes at Alex and plonked himself down next to his brother on the sofa.

I walked past them and took a seat in the armchair, waiting for him to tell me what he obviously couldn't trust me with. I hated that today had now made me question everything that he ever said to me. How could he be falling for me but not able to trust me enough to talk to me about his problems?

"Talk," I ordered when he just stared at me. "Now."

"No," he answered me stubbornly. "This is nothing to do with you."

I stared at his eyes, hating the cold glaze that had come over his chocolate orbs.

"I have shared everything with you," I whispered. "Do you know how hard it has been to open myself back up to another person? To lower the walls and let you in? I really thought that you meant everything that you said to me the other night."

Before I could get the will to stand and leave, his voice rang out, stopping me cold.

"I will lose you," he choked out. "If I tell you this, I will lose you forever." He stared at me for a few moments before he looked at James and nodded his head to the door.

He nodded, clapping him on the shoulder and walked out of the apartment, leaving us both alone.

"Why don't you trust me?" I asked.

"I do! I do trust you but this..." He rubbed his

forehead. "When I tell you this, I won't stop you when you walk out that door. I won't stop you."

I stared at him, not saying a word. I had a feeling that whatever I could have said, wouldn't have sounded right.

"When I was in prison, I shared a cell with this guy called Anton. Anton Giovanni. He was a popular guy and he looked out for me. He brought me into his circle and I had an easier time in prison than I probably would have."

"I'm assuming that he didn't do it out of the goodness of his heart," I muttered.

"Not really. If he looked out for you, it was because he needed something from you. I worked for him. Collected debts, organised beat downs, helped pass drugs from cell to cell, took part in fights for him... It helped to keep my nose clean and it made sure I got out on time." He stared at the floor, and I knew he was ashamed of what he was admitting.

The man he was describing was a stranger to me. I didn't know that man and I never wanted to.

"Go on," I urged softly.

He nodded his head before leaning his elbows on his knees and framing his face in his hands. The action hid his eyes from me and it broke my heart.

I stood and went to him, taking a seat at his side. I reached up and took his fingers, forcing his gaze back to me. "Go on," I repeated.

"A few weeks before my release, a guard found drugs on me. I was on my way to pass them to a customer a few cells down when he found them on me. I thought Anton was going to be furious with me."

"Was he?" I asked.

"No." He shook his head. "He took the fall for me. Said it was him and that the guard was mistaken." He let out a humourless chuckle. "He served extra time for it, and I got to walk free when my time was done."

"He saved you," I whispered.

"Hardly," he muttered. "I may have walked out of that prison but my debt will never be paid. My soul was marked for hell a long time ago."

He looked up at me and I could see the dread that was reflected back at me.

"The guard that busted me never got to make his statement. He was killed in a hit and run accident after work and never got the chance to report what he saw."

"Alex," I whispered. "That poor man."

"I killed that man, Charlie." His voice shook, and I knew he was close to breaking. "I cost that man his life, and I will never forget it." He stood abruptly before walking to the window. "You can go now," he said, coldly dismissing me.

"What?" Now I was pissed. "You think you can just admit something like that and then dismiss me like a piece of trash?"

"You can't want to stay. Not after..."

"Hey!" I grabbed his arm and spun him to face me. "Do you think that little of me? That I would just leave you when you needed me?"

"It's a lot to take on," he muttered. He reached for me, raising his hand and rubbing his thumb along my cheekbone.

"It is." I grasped his hand, holding it to my cheek. "I haven't exactly been without my own drama." I turned my head and kissed his hand before asking my next question. "What I don't understand is why this is suddenly a huge problem now? What happened?"

He sighed. "Anton is in town. Apparently, your ex went to see him. He bought a gun."

Dread settled in my chest, and I knew that whatever problems we may have had, they were going to get a load worse. Like a hundred times worse.

"So, my psychotic ex that has picked up stalking me as his new hobby is now armed and loaded. Fucking great." I looked up at him, hating the sad smile that he gave me. "You shouldn't have been afraid to tell me. We need to be honest with each other," I reprimanded him.

"I'm sorry." He leaned down and kissed my forehead before pulling back. "I didn't want to lose you because the man that I was."

I smoothed his hair back from his face. He was such a beautiful man, but he carried so many shadows within him. Death, despair and grief were his companions, and I was determined not to lose him to his darkness.

"I'm sorry, Alex."

"What for?" He frowned down at me in confusion.

"Your life was normal before me. Now, you have my crazy ex with a grudge." I felt terrible about it. "I think we should go and see Anton."

"No fucking way." He looked at me in shock.

"I'm not asking." I stood up and grabbed my bag from where it was against the wall. "You either take me or I will go and ask David for the location," I threatened. I stared at him for several moments, waiting on his decision.

Does he stay or do I go?

Just as I began thinking I was on my own, he stood up and grabbed his keys. "Let's go." He nodded his head to the door, urging me through it before following behind me. He stopped to lock the door up and walked with me down the stairs, leading me out through the bar.

"Where are you guys going?" James asked.

"To see Anton," I said. "Watch the bar. We'll be back later."

He smirked at my ordering him around before he rolled his eyes at me.

*W*e spent the next forty-five minutes travelling in a taxi into the seedier side of London. It was quiet in the cab with only the sounds of the radio and the busy streets of the city surrounding us. When the car ride started, I had placed my hand in his and refused to let go. He needed to understand that I was there for him just as he was there for me.

The taxi finally came to a stop, and after paying the driver, we climbed out and looked at the building in front of us. It was old, but the front appeared like it had been remodelled with new windows and doors. It had a sign above in bold, black letters: The Dark Room. There were several bikes parked outside and rock music was playing from inside.

"It's not too late to turn back," he warned me.

"Come on." I pulled on his hand and led him inside.

I walked straight up the bar, hating the way that a few men turned to leer at me. I didn't belong in a place like this, but right then, I couldn't care. I was here for a reason and I wasn't leaving without getting the information that I needed.

"I want to speak to the owner," I said to the man behind the bar.

He had stubble on his face and his arms and neck were covered in tattoos. I was sure he was very popular with the ladies, but I wasn't interested. The only man I cared about was the one that I could feel at my back.

"Not today, princess." He turned away from me, moving a few bottles around before turning back.

"Tell Anton he has a visitor," Alex said. "Tell him it's Alex."

"That's okay," a voice said from behind us. "Follow me."

I turned around and watched a man dressed in a dark navy suit lead us towards the back of the club. I guessed it was Anton. He had a smaller frame than Alex but was just as tall. His walk was confident. We followed him down a corridor, not stopping until he was leading us into a room at the end of the hall.

"Take a seat," he said. He walked around his desk and sat, resting his arms on the wood. "This is a surprise, I must say." He turned to me before giving me a beaming smile. "You must be Alex's lady." He was a charming fucker, I had to give him that.

"I'm Charlie." I smiled when Alex reached for my hand, resting them on his knee.

"What can I do for you, Miss Charlie? I am assuming you came here for something specific."

"I want to know what David had off you." He raised his eyebrows in surprise but I quickly continued before he could say anything. "I want to help him. He needs help and I need to know what I'm dealing with."

"I'm not sure how that concerns me." He cocked an

eyebrow at me before his gaze flickered between me and Alex. "I'm not sure if you're aware but—"

"I'm aware," I interjected. "Alex told me everything." I tightened my grip on Alex's hand. "I know that you and Alex go way back. I don't think you realise what David is going to do with that gun."

Anton looked at Alex before coming back to me. "You don't look too worried," he said.

I was terrified. Sadly, though, I was more scared of David. He wasn't the man I knew. He may have controlled me, but to have a gun and plan on using it was a huge leap from controlling.

"I'm not," I lied. "But if David uses that gun on either of us, who do you think is going to be held responsible? David is losing it. He's not the same man anymore. He'll probably be labelled as a crazy fool, but you are the one who supplied an illegal weapon to someone who plans to use it to possibly harm someone." I could feel Alex watching me and I was surprised that he was remaining quiet. "If you can get that gun back," I bargained, "I won't go to the police."

He rested his chin in his hands, staring at me. Suddenly, a smirk appeared on his face before he spoke.

"I like you. You have some guts, I'll give you that. Not many people threaten to drop me in to the police."

"I'm not threatening," I replied. "I need David to move on, and he can't exactly do that when he's going around waving a gun, can he?"

He stared at Alex for several moments before Alex subtly nodded his head.

"I'll sort it," Anton replied. "One-time deal only."

"Why?" I asked, unable to stop myself.

He nodded his head to the door, hinting at us for us to go, refusing to answer me. "It's been a pleasure, Miss Chase." His words were kind but his tone wasn't. "Alex..." He rolled his eyes at me. "Good luck with that one."

We quickly exited the club before walking down the street, arm in arm.

"That went better than I thought."

He slung his arm around my shoulders before kissing the side of my head. "You're awfully sexy when you're bossing hitmen around." He laughed, his warm breath washing over my cheek.

"Do you think he will keep his word?" I bit my lip, worrying.

"Anton is a shitty person, but he doesn't break his word. If he says he's going to do something, he'll do it."

CHAPTER
Twenty

Alex

It had been several weeks since Charlie and I had seen Anton, and I was happy to say that it had been several weeks of complete peace. We hadn't seen David hanging around, so it looked like Anton had gotten the gun back. Well, hopefully. I assumed David would have been in here, waving it about by now otherwise.

I looked up, pulled out of my thoughts, when Charlie came through the door.

"I was beginning to think you had forgotten about me." I walked around the bar-top, not wanting a metal surface between us. "Busy today?"

"Very." She stacked the cake boxes on top of the bar before turning her body to face me. "I would have been here earlier, but the college crowd came in, and I didn't want to leave Addie there on her own. We're a staff member short today."

"Do I get you tonight?" I grinned at her before reaching down and palming her arse cheeks.

"Maybe," she teased. She wrapped her arms around my neck, allowing me to lift her up. She wrapped her legs around my hips before she gently rocked against me. "Have you been missing me?"

"Fuck, yes." I trailed my lips down the column of her neck, sucking at her collarbone. "My hand doesn't feel half as good as you wrapped around me."

She gasped at my words as she grasped the back of my hair and yanked my lips up to hers. She thrust her tongue into my mouth before rocking against me.

I stumbled forward, resting her back against the high bar surface. I tightened my grip on her arse cheeks as I thrust my hips against hers.

"Whoa!" James yelled, none too quietly. "Do I need to go back out?"

We both turned our heads to the side, watching as a cheeky smirk appeared on James's face.

"Hi, James," Charlie muttered before she tapped my shoulders, urging me to put her down. As soon as her feet touched the floor, she grabbed a box and slid it down the bar to him. "Would you help me carry these to the kitchen?"

I could see the blush on her cheeks, but she was

trying to be tough and not make it any worse. I glared at James, silently telling him not to make it any worse.

He chuckled before letting her pile him up with boxes, and they both took the desserts into the kitchen. Several moments later, they were both smiling when they came out of the kitchen.

"What are you two looking so happy about?" I asked, wanting to be in on the joke.

"Nothing for you to worry about." Charlie skipped up to me and gave me a quick kiss before she was heading back to the door. "My place later? Addie is going back home to Manchester for the weekend."

"Sure. See you later, darling." I gave her a wink as she went back next door and turned to James. "So?"

"So what?" he asked. He walked past me and kneeled down next to the box of bottles of Budweiser and began refilling the fridge. "Dude," he said, interpreting my silence correctly. "It's a secret."

A small sliver of jealousy shot up my spine before I squashed it.

"Let's just say," he continued, "that you'll find out tonight." He stood back up to his full height before he clapped me on the shoulder as he passed. "I promise, you'll enjoy it."

*T*he day passed by slowly—too fucking slowly.

"Right! I'm going." I moved from behind the bar before turning to face the boys. "Any problems, give me a ring." I looked around, giving the place another look-over and headed to the door. I avoided the looks of a few past fuck buddies, not bothering. It sounded cold but that's all that they were. Fuck buddies.

Charlie was the girl for me, and I was never going to go back to the man I was before she gave me a chance. It sounded shitty to say, but they knew a different Alex. That Alex didn't give a toss who he stepped on or who he shoved aside. Charlie made me a better man, and any mistakes I made in the past needed to stay there.

Standing outside her building, I felt relief when I didn't see David hanging around. After pressing the buzzer a second time, I smiled when I saw Addie walking towards me with her luggage bag.

"Let me take that." I grabbed the bag from her before turning to the taxi that was pulling up to the kerb. "I could have gotten James to drive you to the train station." I put her bag in the boot and opened the door for her.

"That's okay." She stepped into the cab before giving me a small wave. "Have fun tonight."

"You know something I don't?" I asked.

"Maybe." She turned to the driver. "Victoria Train Station, please."

I reached into my back pocket, pulling a fifty-pound note out before handing it to her through the window.

"Stay safe, beautiful," I called to her before descending the stairs.

She looked surprised at my gesture, but before she could say anything else, the car pulled away from the kerb, taking her to her destination.

I grabbed the door as a young man exited the building, running up the stairs. I knocked on the door, smiling when Charlie opened it.

"Come in. You just missed Addie."

"I just saw her. She was getting into a taxi." I leaned down and kissed her lips before pulling back. "Is there a reason she's going home?" I trailed my eyes down over her outfit, loving how sexy she looked in her white summer dress.

She turned away and led me to the kitchen. "She hasn't been home in a long time. It's her mother's birthday tomorrow, so she thought she'd go home and surprise her." She sounded a little sad by the end of her sentence.

"Hey." I reached for her hand before pulling her to face me. "What's wrong?"

"It's nothing." She shook her head. "I'm just being a stupid girl."

"No, you're not. What is it?"

"I just miss my mum. I haven't seen her in over a year." She shrugged her shoulders. "I've been meaning to go home, but it's just been so crazy here."

"Tell you what. When Addie comes back, we'll plan a time to go and see her. You can even have James to help her in the shop."

"You'd come with me?" She sounded surprised. "Really? To Wales?"

"Yeah." I nodded at her. "It could be fun. I've never been to Wales. Have you told her about us?"

"I may have mentioned some ruggedly handsome bar owner." She giggled. "I spoke to her a few days ago and told her about you. She said she was looking forward to meeting you one day."

"We'll make it happen, darling. I promise." I took a seat at the table, not wanting to crowd her in the kitchen. "So, what are we doing tonight?" I asked.

I hoped that *'stripping her naked and fucking her senseless'* was on the list.

"Well, I thought that as our lives have been *way* too dramatic as of late, that maybe we could do something boring like Netflix and chill." She bent down to the oven and pulled a plate of nachos and cheese out. "Take this into the lounge," she said, handing me the plate, "and I'll be right in."

I did as she asked, kicking my shoes off and taking a seat on the sofa. I grinned when I saw that she had already set us up with some bottles of Budweiser. I grabbed the remote off the table, loaded up her profile and started nosing through her previously watched programmes.

"I'm seeing a theme here," I said when she walked into the lounge.

"Hey! Don't knock Vin Diesel." She put a small plate of chicken wings between us before she took her seat, leaving the seat in between us for the food. She grabbed the remote off me before going to *Fast & Furious 7*. "Fancy it?"

"Sure." I grabbed my bottle, taking a swig and reached for a nacho. I offered it to her, grinning at the look of surprise that was on her face. She parted her lips, allowing me to feed her before eating the cheesy nachos. She did the same for me, gasping when I grabbed her hand, licking the taste off the tips of her fingers.

We spent the rest of the meal, feeding each other bits of nacho and chicken.

After depositing the dishes in the dishwasher, she cuddled up to me, placing her head on my chest and watching Vin Diesel and Paul Walker chase the white lines on the road.

"So, I spent almost all of today trying to ignore what James has been keeping from me." I looked down at her, chuckling at the smile that I saw there.

"I knew you'd forgotten." She bit her lip. "It's not a

big deal. I mean, I know it hasn't exactly been smooth sailing for us."

"Forgotten?" I asked, acting confused before smiling at her. "I wouldn't forget our three month anniversary."

"You remembered!" she shrieked before kneeling up at my side. "We all thought you had forgotten with all the stress you've had lately over Anton."

"Absolutely not." I reached into my jean pocket and pulled the small white jewellery box out. "For you," I said, holding it out for her.

"But I didn't get you anything." She looked so surprised.

"I don't need anything." I grinned when she reached for the box.

"This must have been expensive," she whispered, spotting the *Pandora* logo stamped on the lid of the box.

"Open it," I said, feeling impatient. I had spent over an hour at the shop picking this ring out and I was worried that she wouldn't like it.

She did as I demanded before bringing her hand up to her chest. "Oh, Alex." She pulled the ring out, gazing down at it before turning her watery eyes up to mine. "It's so beautiful." It was a gold ring with a white daisy sitting on top of it. It hadn't been cheap, but she was worth it.

"Well, daisies are your favourite, and I thought..." I stopped talking when she shook her head and slipped the ring on her middle finger. I was relieved when it went straight on.

"It's perfect!" She took my face in her hands and pressed her lips to mine. "It's so beautiful. Thank you so much."

I reached for her and placed her sideways across my lap before blowing out a sigh of relief. "I was nervous you were going to hate it."

"It's so thoughtful of you." She stroked her fingers into the curls at the back of my hair. "I love it. It was so sweet of you to get me something like this."

Before I could say anything, she moved her lips to mine, sucking on my bottom one before slipping her tongue into my mouth. She moved her tongue against mine, moaning when I reached over and fondled her breast.

"Make love to me," she whispered.

Make love. Fuck, I wasn't sure I could do that, but I was willing to give it a try for her.

I nodded my head, steadying her as she stood. I took her hand, following her as she turned the television off and went into the bedroom before closing her door. She moved around me before coming back to standing in front of me. She reached up and grasped my top button and slowly undid them. Her hands shook as she did it, showing how nervous she was. As she undid the bottom button, she slid her hands up over my shoulders and moved the shirt back off my shoulders. As soon as my upper torso became bare for her, she reached up, trailing kisses over my left pectoral.

I dropped my hands, pulling the shirt off before tossing it to the floor. I reached down and placed my hands on her lower back and trailed them further down to where her dress hung down past her waist. I stared into her eyes, silently asking for her permission.

She slowly nodded her head before lifting her hands in the air, urging me to remove it.

I grasped the skirt and slowly pulled it up over her body. I could feel myself growing harder with every patch of skin that was displayed to me. I tossed the dress aside before reaching down and palming her arse cheeks. She was left in a yellow thong and matching bra that was squeezing her tits together in the most delicious cleavage.

She wrapped her arms around my neck at the same time as I lifted her.

We both moaned when she wrapped her legs around my waist. She rocked her hips, causing friction between us.

"Make love to me," she whispered.

CHAPTER
Twenty-One

Charlie

"Make love to me."

His beautiful brown eyes looked up at mine, and it broke me a little at the uncertainty that I could see reflected back at me.

"You look nervous," I whispered. I rested my hand on his shoulder, rubbing my fingers gently along the muscle, attempting to soothe him with my touch. "What is it?"

He swallowed heavily. "Making love is new to me." His grasp tightened where he was holding me. "I don't want to break you."

"You won't." I leaned my head down to his, resting our foreheads together. "You won't hurt me."

He walked us closer to the bed before climbing atop

the mattress. He laid us down in the centre of the bed, resting his weight over mine. He moved his mouth down and trailed kisses along my neck.

I tilted my hips, attempting to rock myself against him, stopping when I realised he was holding back from me.

"I want you," I whispered.

"I know."

He moved down my body, kissing down between my cleavage and stomach. He slid his fingers under the straps of my thong on my hips before he tugged. I lifted my hips, allowing him to pull them down my legs. He tossed them over his shoulder behind him as he lay down between my legs, parting them wide enough for his shoulders.

"I've been thinking about doing this to you all fucking day," he gritted out. He moved his face closer to me before he kissed the inside of my leg. My hips shot up, making him chuckle.

"Sensitive, darling?" He turned his head and did the same to the other leg before he sucked my clit into his mouth. He moved his tongue down further, licking up my slit.

I moaned at the contact, waiting for him to do it again. I wasn't kept waiting long.

He moaned against me, causing sparks to explode inside of me. I rocked my hips against his face, gasping when I felt him tilt my pelvis up to his mouth. His tongue began moving faster as I felt him press a finger to my opening. He slid two digits inside me straight away before adding a third. He pumped them inside me slowly before he sped up.

"Fuck, stop," I gasped. "I'm going to come if you keep that up."

"Fuck, yes."

He flicked his tongue harder against me, not stopping until I was coming apart for him, calling out his name.

"I'll never get tired of hearing you call out my name." He climbed off the bed before undoing his jeans. He grabbed a condom out of his pocket and I sat up, stopping him.

"I'm clean," I blurted out. "I'm on the pill. If you wanted to..."

He stared at me for a moment before he pulled his jeans down, dropping them on the floor.

"If you're sure," he whispered.

I parted my legs for him, moaning when I felt his hard length nudge against me. He slipped his hands beneath me and unclasped my bra, before tossing it aside.

"I need to feel you," he whispered. "All of you." He reached down and lined himself up with me, gently moving inside of me.

I moaned, arching my back, feeling the pleasure spike.

"Fuck!" he gasped. "You feel so good." He moved further inside of me, increasing the speed of his thrusts. "So fucking good." He leaned his weight on his hands on either side of me, watching my breasts move from his position.

I lifted my hands and trailed them up over his shoulders before grasping the back of his neck and pulling his forehead down to mine.

"I..." I stopped, unsure of how to say it—unsure how to say what I had vehemently denied for the last few weeks.

He stopped moving, his eyes widening in surprise. He knew.

"I love you," I whispered. "I really do."

He pushed his face down to mine before thrusting his tongue in between my parted lips. He moaned against my mouth before his hips began moving against mine again.

"Fuck, I love you, too." He moved his lips harder against mine before he dipped his head, sucking my nipple into his mouth. His grip on my hip tightened as I felt him start to tense. "Come for me, baby. Come for me now." He reached up and grasped my breast, pulling roughly on my nipple. His hips sped up, thrusting harder before I felt pleasure explode through me.

I moaned against his lips, clenching my legs around his hips when I felt his orgasm hit. He slumped against me, crushing me with his weight before I felt him turn his head and kiss the side of my neck behind my ear.

"Fuck me," he gasped. He rolled over, slipping out of me and pulled me against his side.

"I think I just did that." I pressed a kiss to his chest before entwining my legs with his.

"You did." He dipped his head and kissed the top of my head. "It's never felt like that before." He grinned down at me.

"No," I whispered. "It hasn't."

"Do you feel okay?" he asked, looking down at me.

"I feel great. A little sticky." I wiggled my hips before continuing. "I feel happy."

He stared down at me for a moment before he dipped his head, kissing my lips gently.

"So do I, darling." He tightened his arm around me before taking my other hand in his and resting it over his chest. "So do I."

*W*alking up the next morning, I opened my eyes, unable to stop smiling at the sight that greeted me.

Alex was lying on his side, facing me. He had the cutest pout on his face and had his arm loosely wrapped across my waist. He had been perfect last night, and falling asleep in his arms after our evening together was the perfect ending to an already perfect anniversary.

I could have laid there all morning watching him, but unfortunately, the clock behind Alex was taunting me with the time. I gently moved his arm, being careful not to wake him, and shuffled out of bed. I was due at the café, especially as Addie wasn't here to help.

After taking a shower, I dried my hair in the kitchen, mindful of how loud my hairdryer could be. Tossing it up in a sloppy bun, I snuck into my bedroom and threw on a clean uniform before scribbling a note down and leaving it on the side for him.

Loved waking up with you. Hope you'll keep me warm tonight – C xxx

Walking into the café, I groaned when I realised I was only half-hour early before the doors would open. I quickly grabbed an apron, and after washing my hands, I whipped up a cookie batch. I was just scooping uneven blobs onto the cookie sheets when Sandra walked in through the door.

"I'm so sorry I'm late!" She grabbed an apron from the back of the door and tied it around her waist. "Is it just me and you today?" she asked, looking around.

"Yes." I popped two trays of cookies in the oven before turning to her. "Addie has gone to visit her parents in Manchester so it's going to be busy today."

"No problem. I'll be out front if you need me."

The day slowly passed, and I was a little disappointed that Alex hadn't been by to see me. It was selfish because I knew how busy his bar got, and I knew he had been working the days and relying on his staff to cover the nights so he could spend time with me.

That evening I went straight to the bar, not wanting to be alone. I stopped by for a kiss, loving the look of surprise on his face.

"How was your day?"

"It was good. It's busy here," I said, looking around. "Is it cool if I stay with you tonight?"

"Of course it is." He frowned at me before reaching out and sliding his finger along my cheekbone. "You look tired."

"I am." I gave a small wave to James.

"I, uh, I can't escape for another few hours. One of the boys rang in sick," he apologised.

"That's okay." I went to take a step away but he stopped me by holding his key out for me. "I'll be up when we close up most likely."

"You trust me in your home unsupervised?" I teased. I was oddly touched that he was letting me stay.

"Of course. I have Netflix and Prime so make yourself at home." He grinned at me. "What do you want to eat? I can bring it up when it's ready."

"Oooh. Can I have a steak sandwich and fries, please?"

James nodded before going to move past us.

"And maybe some onion rings and a strawberry shake?" I cheekily added on.

"Damn, woman. You can eat." James laughed as he went to the kitchen.

"You haven't eaten today, have you?" Alex asked, concerned.

"No." I shook my head, avoiding his frown. "It's been too busy."

"Okay." He tapped my hand and nodded his head behind him to the staircase. "Go on up."

I held his key tighter in my hand and made my way upstairs. His scent was everywhere, and it relaxed me immediately. I went into his bedroom and grabbed his t-shirt that was on the end of his bed. I picked it up, loving how it still smelled of him. I quickly stripped and slipped it over my head. It swamped me and hung to just above my knees.

Taking a seat on the sofa, I loaded his extremely large television up. After browsing through his apps, I giggled when I saw that he had Disney+. I selected *Avengers Endgame* and waited for it to load up. I would always be Team Bucky and Cap. Those two were fucking hot together.

"Room service!" a voice called from the door, and Alex came in, carrying my food and shake on a serving tray.

"I could get used to this!" I sat up, smiling up at him as he placed the tray on my lap.

"I hope so!" He bent down and pressed his lips roughly to mine. "You look so fucking sexy in my top." He groaned, pulling away from me. "Don't tease." He palmed his cock, rearranging his hardness. "I'd rather be up here between your legs than down there."

"Well, you have my permission to wake me up however you like when you come up." I blew him a kiss as he turned away and started walking to the door.

"I'll hold you to that, minx." He gave me his signature wink before he disappeared downstairs.

I giggled, grabbing a fry and dipping it into my shake, moaning at the mixed taste of salty and sweet. Addie usually called me a pig when I did that.

The movie ended with me a sobbing mess. It was a perfect ending and one that was needed. I reached for the remote and turned the television off before taking the dishes to the kitchen and washing them clean. Stacking them on the worktop to take down to James's kitchen tomorrow, I walked to the bedroom, leaving the light on in the lounge for Alex. I quickly climbed under the blanket, snuggling into Alex's pillow, inhaling his scent as sleep sucked me under, where I remained until morning.

CHAPTER
Twenty-Two

Alex

"Lock up on your way out, James." I tossed a few glass bottles in the bin after cleaning the tables and headed to the staircase. "I'll see you tomorrow, bro." I walked into the apartment, expecting to see Charlie on the sofa, but there was no sign of her. I passed the kitchen, grinning when I saw she had cleaned up after herself. I kicked my shoes off and walked to the bedroom.

Standing at the door, I stood there for a few moments, watching her lying in my bed. She was in the middle, cuddling her head into my pillow. She had kicked the blankets off, showing her beautiful, creamy legs. She looked fucking perfect. Watching her lying there, taking up my space, I knew it was a sign that I wanted her forever.

I pulled my top off, tossing my jeans aside and climbed into bed behind her. I didn't want to disturb her too much. I wrapped my arm over her waist before dropping my head to her hair and inhaling her strawberry scent.

She moaned sleepily before turning her head. "Hi."

"Hi, yourself." I kissed her cheek before bringing her closer to my chest.

"You're so warm," she sleepily muttered.

"That was the deal, right?" I asked, reminding her back to the note she had left me this morning.

"Right," she giggled. "I love falling asleep with you."

"Me too, darling." I kissed her forehead before laying my head back. "Sweet dreams."

*A*fter spending a good portion of the night staring at the ceiling, I was surprised to wake up in the morning to the smell of bacon. I climbed out of bed, pulling on a pair of grey jogger bottoms and walked out to the kitchen.

"Something smells yummy." I chuckled when I saw how much she had cooked: bacon, eggs, pancakes, waffles, toast, juice... "Now *this* I could get used to." I wrapped an arm around her waist and tugged her into me before rocking my hips against her arse.

She gasped, lifting her arms and placing them behind my neck, threading her fingers into the back of my hair. She tilted her head, pressing her lips to mine before pulling back and focusing her attention back on the stove.

"You're distracting me," she admonished. "Fill your plate and I'll be there in a minute."

I kissed the skin on her shoulder from where my t-shirt had fallen down a little. After plating up some pancakes and bacon, I poured us some glasses of cranberry juice and took a seat at the table. She didn't keep me waiting long before she joined me with a waffle and sliced strawberries. We settled down to a quiet breakfast, talking about the café mostly. As she forked up the last of her strawberries, feeding me a couple, I took her hand, rubbing my thumb over the back of it.

"Is everything okay?" she asked. "You were a bit fidgety last night."

I sighed. "It's nothing." I shook my head. "Nothing for you to worry about."

"Oh." She dipped her head, focusing her gaze on a scratch in the wooden table before continuing. "I thought… I thought we had moved past this." She still wouldn't look at me.

"I'm sorry," I apologised. "I, uh, I wanted to ask you something."

"Okay." She tightened her hand around mine before nodding her head at me to continue. "I'm listening."

"When I got home last night you were already in bed. I stood at the doorway watching you sleep for a little," I said, pointing at the doorway to my bedroom. I could tell by her expression I was confusing her. A small blush started to bloom on her cheeks.

"I thought how perfect you looked lying there in my bed. That I wanted to keep seeing it."

"I love being here with you," she whispered. "I feel so comfortable with you. It feels like we were always meant to get to this place."

"Yeah." I blew out a sigh, needing to say this next part and get it out. "I know this is fast, but I want to live with you. I want to share it all with you."

Her eyes widened in surprise at me. "Alex…"

"Let me finish," I said, shaking my head. "I know we have a long way to go, and I know we don't know every little thing there is to know about each other, but I think we've come through the worst. I want to find out the rest. I want to see your mood swings, I want to wake up with you wrapped around me and your crazy hair in my face. I want to see you when you get the munchies and stuffing your face with chocolate. I want to be the one who dries your tears when you cry and who laughs with you when you get hysterical. I want it all."

Her eyes glistened up at me and I hoped to fuck

they were happy tears. I hoped to fuck I wasn't scaring her the hell away from me. "Well, you're not running out of the apartment yet, so I'm hoping that's a good thing," I joked.

"I don't know what to say," she whispered. "It's just a little fast and I…"

"I know it's fast," I agreed. "Super fast." We both chuckled at my lack of articulation. "I just know I want you with me whenever I can have you, and I'm kind of hoping that it's the same for you."

"It is. Of course, it is, Alex." She blew out a shaky breath. "What if it doesn't work out? What if it's just one step too far, too fast?"

"It might be," I answered, "but I don't think it will be." I reached over and trapped her hand between my palms. "I think, the question that you need to ask yourself is, do you want this as much as I do?"

She stared at me for a few moments before she looked down at her lap.

I mentally chastised myself, knowing full well what words were going to come out of her mouth next. It was too fucking fast and I was pressuring her—something I warned myself I would never fucking do.

"Okay." She looked up at me, surprising the fucking hell out of me. "Okay, let's do it."

"What?" I laughed, surprised. "You're serious?"

"Yes!" A beaming smile took over her face. "I'm not the easiest person to live with, mind—I'm messy, always leave my dirty clothes on the floor and you'll be finding hair-ties all over the place—but if you want me…"

"Fuck, yes, I want you." I pulled her hand to my lips, pressing kisses to the back of it.

We both stood and she threw her arms around my neck, kicking her legs behind her, hugging me before placing them back down.

"I love you," she whispered. She leaned up and pressed her lips to mine before pulling back.

"I love you too, darling." I placed my hands on her hips, squeezing them gently before stepping back. "Celebratory drink down in the bar tonight?"

"Can we wait?" she asked. She bit her lip, staring at my chest before meeting my eyes again. "I want to tell Addie first. Is that okay?"

"Of course. Do you think she'll take it okay?"

"She will. It'll just be better if I tell her first." She reached for my hands, squeezing them gently. "She's due back this evening, so I'll take her out for some drinks. She and I haven't done that in a while."

"Bring her to the bar," I suggested. "You girls can have some food and cocktails. Maybe it'll help wake James up."

"You still think something is going on?" She looked at me with doubt. "You'd make a terrible matchmaker."

"I got you, didn't I?" I teased her. "Worked out good there."

"True." She pulled away from me. "I had better get home and get a fresh uniform before work."

"Go." I grabbed the dishes from the table. "I'll wash up. See you tonight." Another kiss to her luscious lips and she was leaving me to the dishes.

Well, she did say she was messy. Can't say she didn't warn me on that one.

"You're freaking me out!" James admonished. "Why are you smiling like that?"

"Like what?" I asked, serving a round of drinks up before delivering them to a family of five.

"Like *that!*" He pointed at me, laughing. "You've been walking around with a goofy smile on your face all damn bastard day! Even the customers have noticed. Is Charlie that good at—?"

I cut him off by delivering a hard punch to his arm, making him wince. "Finish that sentence and you'll have trouble fucking walking tomorrow," I threatened.

"My bad." He raised his hands in defence. "It was only a joke, man."

"I know. She's just more than that, you know? She's special, man."

"I can see that." He nodded his head. "That's cool. It's good to see you happy, Alex. You both deserve it." He chuckled before moving past me. "Just let me know when I need to get something blue or pink." He clapped me on the shoulder, laughing before disappearing to the end of the bar.

"That's not funny," I admonished him. "Not fucking funny, at all."

CHAPTER
Twenty-Three

Charlie

"So, how was your mum?" I asked Addie. "Did you do any shopping? Ooh, what were the theatres like? Did you meet up with any friends while you were home?" I was rambling now. "Did she enjoy her birthday?"

"Whoa!" She held her hands up, her new gel nails catching my eye. "What's with all the questions?"

"Nothing." I shrugged my shoulders before stealing a fry off her plate. "Just interested in how your weekend went."

"Okay. Well, Mum was great—happy to see me home. Yes to shopping. I didn't go to any theatres, I'm afraid, and no to seeing friends. I just hung out with Mum and we got our nails done." She held her hands out for me to admire her professional-looking manicure.

"Ooh, lovely!" I complimented. "I can never grow mine."

"Because you keep biting them." She lightly tapped my hand. "Now, tell me what's going on."

"Uh, what do you mean?" I asked, acting confused. There's no way she could know.

"Alex keeps looking over here. Look at him! He looks like he's having his balls squeezed in a vice." We both giggled at her description, and after staring over at him, I decided he did look a little uncomfortable.

"Something has happened, but I'm not sure how you're going to take it." I pulled a face, letting my nerves take hold for a moment.

"Just spit it out." She crossed her arms on the table-top before reaching over and placing her hand on my lower arm. "It's me. Whatever it is, you know I'll be okay." Her eyes flicked down before her eyes widened in surprise. "Holy crap! Are you pregnant?"

"No!" I laughed at how ridiculous that thought was. "Absolutely not."

"Oh." She slumped back in her seat, her shoulders falling in disappointment. "Then what is it?" She took a sip of her cosmopolitan cocktail before nodding for me to continue.

"Alex has asked me to move in with him." I pulled a face, waiting for her response.

She stared at me for a few moments in silence before a beaming smile took over her face and she shot to her feet, letting out a major squeal.

I stood, laughing at her when she wrapped her arms around my neck, hugging me tightly and rocking us from side to side.

"I'm so happy for you!" she shrieked. "How would you think I'd take that badly?" She lightly tapped me on my upper arm before grabbing it and pulling me over to the bar. "Come here you!" She held her arms out and walked through the gap in the bar before pulling Alex down into a hug.

"You're happy for us!" He grinned down at her, giving her a quick kiss on the cheek.

"What's going on?" James asked from behind Alex.

"Charlie and Alex are moving in together!" Addie shrieked, bouncing on the spot and clapping her hands enthusiastically.

"Are you pregnant?" James asked, looking over at me.

"No!" Alex and I shouted at the same time. We both laughed at our timing before I continued. "No. Don't wish that on us."

Alex came around the bar and wrapped his arm around my waist, bending down and kissing my temple. "That didn't go too bad." He trailed his fingers over the top of my arm before he bent his head and whispered in my ear. "You are looking very fuckable in this sparkly dress."

I gasped before patting his chest, silently admonishing him.

"So, uh…" Addie leaned her elbows on the bar-top, looking between us. "What's happening with David?"

"I haven't seen him lately."

Alex shook his head, agreeing with me and I was thankful for that—thankful that neither of us had seen him hanging around. Maybe it was a sign that he was moving on.

"Interesting." She grinned at Alex. "I thought Charlie was going to tell me she was knocked up."

James laughed loudly. "I said the same thing earlier." He grinned as he filled a pint glass with cider for a customer from the pump. "He had a goofy grin on his face and I thought—"

"Thank you!" I said loudly, pretty much cutting him off from finishing that sentence. "Anyway, let's toast a drink."

"Yes!" Addie cheered. She reached behind her and grabbed a bottle of vodka before lining up four shots. We each grabbed one and waited for her to announce what we were toasting to. "To family!" she cheered, holding her shot glass up.

We all clinked our glasses, knocking them back, and I couldn't help the cough that came from the burn that went down my throat.

Addie giggled at my face before she filled another shot and knocked it back. She was a professional at drinking vodka. No cough came from her.

She gave me a cocky smirk and placed the bottle back on the shelf and coming back around to the bar. "So, what else have I missed while I've been out of town?"

"Nothing much."

Alex went back behind the bar and Addie and I strolled back to our seats. James came over with another round of cocktails before leaving us to chat.

"I have been thinking about closing the shop on Sundays," I admitted.

"How come?" She stirred her drink with a straw and took a pull.

"It's manic through the week, and I thought it'd be nice to have a day off. It's been easier using suppliers for a few of the baked products." I shrugged my shoulders. "Plus, Alex said he would come home with me to Wales one weekend and visit Mum."

"Meeting the parents!" she teased. "Pretty serious."

"Yeah." I looked over at him and watched as he handed a straw to a little girl. She couldn't have been older than ten years. "It never felt like this with David. With him, there was no..." I struggled to find the right word, stopping when Addie interrupted me.

"Love." She raised her eyebrows at me, daring me

to disagree. "You cared for him, but I don't think that you ever truly loved him."

I stared at her, a little surprised by her conclusion.

I did love David, didn't I?

"I saw you after he'd fucked his receptionist. You were sad but you weren't broken." She reached over and took my hand in hers. "You never looked at David the way you look at Alex. Your eyes twinkle when you look at him. I never saw that when you and David were together."

"No wonder he hates me," I whispered, feeling ashamed.

"He doesn't hate *you*," she said. "He hates that he couldn't control you," she explained further. "On the crime documentaries I watch..."

"Here we go," I mocked. "Those crime documentaries will send you crazy, you know that, right?"

"Listen! These stalkers and nut-jobs as you call them, they need to have a victim. Someone they can control. I'm not saying he was a stalker when you two were together, but I think there was a part of you that he was controlling." She lowered her head to catch my avoiding gaze. "I remember all the put-downs, the dismissive comments, the dates he missed, the many voicemail messages that were always left on our machine..." She tightened her hand in mine. "You deserve better than that, sweetheart. And that"—she nodded her head towards the bar—"*that* is better." We both smiled at each other before she continued. "And really fucking hot."

We both giggled as we clinked our glasses together. We stayed at the bar for a couple more drinks before we made our way home. Alex offered me to stay with him, but I decided to go home with Addie, not wanting our girly night to end just then.

A few weeks slowly passed before I moved out of my apartment with Addie. I had decided to stay another month, not wanting to leave her with an extra bill to pay to cover my rent. We were lucky though because a friend of Addie's, Kelly, from the club that she used to dance at needed a place to stay, and so when I moved out, she moved in.

It didn't take me long to move in. Alex was a sweetheart and helped me unpack all of my boxes and even made space in his wardrobe for me. The only thing that I had left to unpack was my books, but those would have to wait until Alex sorted me a bookcase. He promised to set one up for me this weekend.

I occasionally had moments when I felt like we were still moving a little too fast but it often felt like Alex had gotten to know me well enough to know when those moments of panic happened. He'd usually take the afternoon off or surprise me by cooking me dinner when I got home from the café.

I shook my head, clearing my thoughts from my latest freak-out. The last couple of days I had started feeling unwell. At first, I thought that Alex had given me food poisoning, but I wasn't stupid. I secretly knew what it was, and I was freaking out. Massively.

In situations like this where I am going nuts, I would normally call Addie. I want her to hold my hand while I peed on a stick, but I couldn't. I had to put my trust in the person I was sharing a home with. I had to be an adult about this.

I reached for my phone and sent a text message to Alex, asking him to come upstairs. It was Tuesday evening, so I was hoping it was slow enough for him to be able to escape. Minutes later, he was coming through the door, a look of worry on his face.

"What is it?" he asked. He took a seat on the sofa next to me and rested his hand on my knee. "What's wrong?" He dipped his head to look in my eyes. "What's with the tears?"

"I've done something really stupid," I whispered.

His face dropped before he leaned back a little. He looked shocked at my outburst, and I knew how it must have sounded to him.

"What do you mean?" he asked. "Are you regretting...?" He left the question open, waiting for me to fill in the blanks.

"No, I'm not." I reached for his hand, entwining our fingers. "I'm happy here. It's just..." I sighed, not knowing how to say it. "Come with me." I pulled him with me, leading him to the bathroom. I pointed my finger to the sink where I'd left the pregnancy stick, waiting for his response. I really had no clue how he was going to take this. I wanted him to be okay with it, but I was also worried he was going to flip out. Having me move in was one thing, but having me *and* a baby might be one thing too many.

I watched as his shoulders tensed and I cringed, waiting for him to start yelling.

"Is this?" His hand shook when he picked up the test, staring down at it.

"It's positive," I whispered. "I'd have to go to the doctors to confirm it but I've taken three different ones and they all say..." I stopped talking when he spun around before his eyes flicked down to my stomach. I expected to see anger or hesitation in his gaze but there was none. Instead, his eyes glistened at me as he marched forward. He bent down and slipped his hands behind my knees and he lifted me up into his arms and spun us in a circle, carrying me Cinderella-style.

"What are you doing?" I shrieked, caught off guard by his actions.

"There's really a little life inside of you." His eyes went down to my stomach before coming back to my eyes.

I slipped my arms around his shoulders, smiling up at him, feeling relieved. "There is," I whispered. "I was afraid to tell you but I..." I swallowed past the lump in my throat, trying to form my words. "We're always honest with each other, and I didn't want to keep anything from you."

During my speech, he had begun walking us to the sofa. He sat me down on the sofa and kneeled down in front of me. He placed his hand on my stomach over my t-shirt before he looked up at me, a beaming smile taking over his expression. "I'm happy about this," he confessed. "Are you?"

"I think so," I whispered. "*This* is definitely fast." We both chuckled. "But it feels right. You, me and bump feels right."

He leaned forward and dipped his head before lifting my t-shirt. He pressed a kiss to just above my belly button, tickling the skin there.

"I'll be good to you," he whispered. "To you both."

"I know you will." I stroked my fingers into his hair, smoothing it back and away from his face. "This will be a learning curve for us both."

"When do you want to tell people?" he asked.

"I have a doctor's appointment tomorrow. Just for them to assign me a midwife, I guess." I smiled as he stroked his fingers over my stomach. "I'd like us to wait until I'm past twelve weeks."

He frowned at my answer. "I don't know," he hedged. "You work in that café too hard."

I giggled at how worried he was sounding already. "I'm pregnant, Alex!" I admonished. "Pregnant women can still work."

"We'll have to get you a stool or something for the kitchen."

"We'll see," I said, placating him. "Let's see how I go at the doctor's go tomorrow and we can go from there."

———

*A*lex was the perfect gentleman and came to my appointment with me. He held my hand as we waited for the results. When they confirmed that we were expecting, he was impossible to calm down. The smile could *not* be wiped off his face, and I knew that he was just as excited for this baby as I was.

The weeks slowly passed, and by the time I made it to twelve weeks, Alex was like a firework ready to explode. We had decided to keep the announcement small, so on Monday evening, I had dinner down at the bar. There weren't many customers in: only a couple of families celebrating birthdays and engagements.

It had been difficult keeping it from Addie but I'd wanted it to be a surprise. I had become super emotional over the last couple of weeks, and I knew

Addie was probably suspecting that there was something going on.

"You ready?" He leaned his elbows on the bar-top, pinching a fry off of my plate before dipping it in the sauce. "You haven't touched that burger in the last ten minutes."

"I'm nervous." I looked past him where Addie stood at the jukebox, laughing at something James was saying.

"Do you have butterflies?" he teased.

"More like moths." We both laughed at my description before he came around the bar and took my hand in his.

"Ladies and gents, I'm sorry to interrupt your evenings." He took a few steps forward, pulling me with him. "We have a little announcement that we'd like to share."

I looked at Addie, smiling at the look on her face. She had her arm looped through James's and was bouncing a little in her stand.

"Charlie and I are happy to announce..." A moment's pause. "We are having a baby!"

A round of applause erupted amongst the customers but it was quickly drowned out by Addie's squeals. She came running toward us, arms wide open, and pulled us both down to a hug before she planted kisses on both of our cheeks.

"I'm going to be an auntie!" she shrieked, looking like the female smurf. She jumped up and down, clapping her hands before she pulled me back into her arms—a solo hug this time. "I'm so happy for you, Charlie!"

My eyes filled when I saw Alex being hugged by James, both giving manly thumps to each other's backs.

I pulled back from Addie, smiling when she went straight to Alex and gave him the same treatment that she'd given me. Seconds later, James was pulling me into a hug, giving me a kiss on the cheek before stepping back.

"So, what are you having?" he asked.

"We've decided to keep it a surprise," Alex said, placing his arm around my shoulders before pulling me into his side.

"Free drinks!" James yelled to the bar before disappearing behind it. Moments later, everyone had a glass in their hands, toasting the new addition to our families.

"Congrats to Alex and Charlie!" he cheered.

Everyone toasted their glasses and I was filled with a deep sense of warmth and love.

Warmth for the future and love for our little baby.

CHAPTER
Twenty-Four

Alex

The weeks passed a lot faster than I would have liked. One day it felt like we were announcing to our world that she was pregnant and the next, she had a bump big enough to give her trouble fitting into her jeans.

"Do you think you're carrying twins?" I asked, teasing her.

She rolled her eyes at me before grabbing the door handle to her mum's house and opening it. We had decided to drive up in James's car. She was just over five months pregnant now and didn't want to chance going on the train. To say I was a nervous wreck would be an understatement.

"Mum! It's me," she called. "We're here!"

"There she is!" A high-pitched shriek came from the back house.

I stepped back as mother and daughter embraced each other. I smiled, watching them hug. Her mum was the same height as Charlie and had grey streaks in her hair. She gave me a smile over Charlie's head and pulled back and smoothed the hair back from her daughter's face before her eyes shot down to the bump.

"Look at you!" She placed her hand on Charlie's bump.

I knew from the beaming smiles on both of their faces that they could feel the baby kicking.

"This is Alex," Charlie said, reaching her hand back for mine. "Alex, this is my mum, Susan."

"Hello, Ms. Chase." I stepped back and shook her hand. "It's lovely to meet you."

She looked up at me, smiling before holding her arms open. "We hug around here, sweetie." She pulled me into an embrace, patting my shoulders before pulling back. "I see they grow them big in London."

"Mum." Charlie giggled.

"I'm only teasing. Put that bag down by there and let's go into the kitchen." She linked her arm with Charlie's and led us through. "Have you ever tasted welsh cakes before, Alex?"

It was a medium-sized kitchen with worktops around the edges of the room and a small, round table on the left by the door. She grabbed a teapot from near the window and took a seat next to Charlie before gesturing for me to take the seat next to her.

"No." I winked at Charlie. "Charlie makes some delicious caramel bites but I don't think she has ever made welsh cakes."

Susan made a clucking noise with her tongue. "And you call yourself a baker," she teased. "Help yourself," she said.

Charlie and I went to grab one at the same time but she beat me to it. She poked her tongue out at me before taking a bite, moaning at the taste. "No one makes them like you, Mum." She darted her eyes to the plate, gesturing for me to take one. "You may love these more than my caramel bites. Mum makes currant ones and ones with chocolate chips."

I took a bite, groaning as the sweetness registered on my taste buds. "These are good." Another two bites and I was finishing it off, quickly reaching for another.

"So, Alex. How did you meet my Charlie?"

"I've known Charlie for a while, to be honest, Ms. Chase. She made me wait for her." I winked at her.

"So, you're a patient man, Alex."

"No." I laughed at her words. "Not at all. But I came to learn that she was worth the wait."

Charlie reached across the table for my hand, smiling at me when I grasped her fingers. "And now we're going to be a family," I continued.

We spent that weekend getting to know each other. I stepped out for a couple of hours on Saturday, seeing the sights of Cardiff so that Charlie and her mum could spend some time together, just the two of them. I knew that these moments were precious for them, and I knew they would be moments that Charlie would cherish when she got back to London. She also wanted to ask her mother to come up and stay for a few days when the baby was born and get to know her grandchild a little and bond. Charlie didn't have any family in London, and I wanted to make it as easy as possible for her. I think I underestimated that it must be sometimes lonely for Charlie when she was on her own. I wanted to be her family, but I could never fill the spot that her mother had. I still missed my mum terribly, and I didn't want Charlie to have to go through that.

That evening we spent time eating Chinese food around the table as Susan poured over childhood memories and photographs of Charlie when she was a little girl.

Later that night, I made my way downstairs to the kitchen, not able to sleep. Rather than disturbing Charlie, I went downstairs for a drink, surprised when I saw Susan sitting at the table, reading a book.

"Can't sleep?" she asked, slipping a bookmark in to mark her place in the book.

"Not really. I thought I'd come down for a glass of water and try again."

"Or," she said, standing up and walking past me to the sink. "You can have a sit-down and tell me what's keeping you awake." She filled a glass with water and came back to me, placing it down in front of me and re-taking her seat. "Are you nervous about the baby coming?"

"No." I shook my head before taking a sip. "Doesn't that sound funny? I should be petrified, shouldn't I?" I twirled the glass in a circle on the spot, fidgeting. "I mean, having a baby is life-changing." A pause. "Right?"

She leaned her elbow on the table and supported her face by placing her hand beneath her chin. "Usually." She raised her eyebrows at me before continuing. "So, if it's not the baby, Alex. What *are* you nervous about?"

She had the same eyes as her daughter. Open. Honest.

I blew out a breath, deciding to share my concern with Charlie's mum. "I want to propose to her." I waited for her to react badly but when she just stared at me, my shoulders slumped with relief. "You don't look surprised."

She laughed at my words before she placed her

hand on mine. "Alex, you and my daughter are having a baby. If you didn't want to make a life with her, I'd be concerned." She tapped my hand before pulling back. "Is that the problem?" she asked, pushing further. "You're afraid that she will say no?"

"No." I frowned. "Yes. Maybe." We both laughed at my flustering. "Charlie is sometimes hard to read. Most of the time, it's so easy to see what she's thinking. Other times..."

"She loves you, Alex." She stood and walked to the sink, emptying her cup. "She spent most of the afternoon talking about you both. How happy she is living with you." She walked back to me before resting her hand on my shoulder. "Ask her. You'll probably find you are worrying over nothing."

I nodded, feeling a little better after her admission.

"Thank you, Susan." I gave her a small wave before going back upstairs and climbing back into bed.

"Where did you go?" Charlie sleepily mumbled.

"Just for a drink." I wrapped my arm around her waist and cuddled her back against my chest, before resting my hand on her bump. "Go back to sleep, darling." I dipped my head and kissed her cheek and lay my head back on the pillow, waiting for sleep to claim me.

After speaking to Susan, it didn't take me long.

e were ready by noon for the drive back home to London. After throwing our bags in the boot, I stood back, trying to give Charlie and her mum some privacy to say goodbye.

Susan kissed her on the cheek before tucking hair back behind Charlie's ears. "We can arrange some dates for me to come and stay," she said.

Charlie nodded at her words.

Susan turned to me. "Thank you for bringing my baby girl back for a visit, Alex." She reached up and pulled me down into a hug. "It's been wonderful to meet you." She kissed my cheek and stepped back. "You take care of her."

"I will." I waited while they hugged again before helping Charlie into the passenger seat. Another wave and we were pulling away from the kerb, starting the drive back to London.

We drove in silence for several moments before Charlie spoke up. "Thank you for coming home with me." She reached across and placed her hand on my leg. "You've been amazing this weekend."

"You're welcome, darling." I reached down and grabbed her hand before pulling it up to my lips for a kiss. "Your mum seems like an amazing woman. It'll be nice for her to come and stay with us for a few days when the baby comes."

"It will," she whispered. "It'll be nice for her to meet James as well and to see Addie again."

"And our beautiful child," I teased.

She giggled. "I can't believe I'm five months already." She placed her hands on her bump before softly rubbing a spot next to her belly button. "Kicking a lot lately."

"That's good, right?" I asked, checking. "I mean, activity is a good thing. That's what it said in the books."

"It is." She leaned her head back against the headrest before closing her eyes. "We are going to be good," she whispered.

"*B*ro! How long are you going to keep carrying that box around?" James gestured to my leg where it was obvious the ring box was in my pocket.

We had been home for a few weeks, and James had come to the jewellery shop closer to the city centre to help pick the ring out with me. I had suggested recruiting Addie and her expertise, but James had quickly shut that down, insisting that Addie wouldn't be able to keep it a secret.

He'd probably been right. She was a very excitable person. Too fucking excitable, sometimes.

"I'm waiting for the right moment." I rolled my eyes at him. "It has to be right. Girls care about that shit."

"*You* are the girl!" He chuckled. "Just take her aside and ask her. It's not difficult." He looked over at me. "Are you afraid she's going to say no?"

Fuck. All his questions were making me edgy. I hadn't been paranoid before but now I fucking was.

"Addie!" I enthusiastically greeted her as she came through the door.

She frowned at me, caught off guard by my enthusiasm. "Where's Charlie?" she asked. She took a seat on the stool before she began fiddling with the drink mats.

"She's upstairs taking a nap." I grabbed a glass and filled it with coke from the pump, popping a straw and a slice of lime in it and placed it in front of her. "Is there a problem?"

Charlie had made Addie assistant manager, and she had taken on more servers in the café. She did some of her baking upstairs when she was having an off day, and Addie usually came by to pick up the treats. She had been having a lot of sick days lately, but she told me that it was nothing to worry about.

"No." She looked away from me.

"Talk," I demanded. "Now."

"I don't want to worry anyone. It's just..." Her shoulders slumped before she continued. "David came into the shop this morning."

"What did he want?" I asked.

"Cookies," she muttered. She rolled her eyes. "He walked up to the counter and asked for a box of cookies. He looked awful. He had bruises on his face."

Sounded like he'd had that visit from Anton's boys.

I stared at her for a few moments, not liking the worry I saw reflected back at me. This was out of character for David, and the last thing any of us needed was David hanging around the place.

"Is that the first time?" I asked, needing to know.

She quickly nodded her head. "Yes, it's the first time."

I relaxed a little at her admission. "If you see him again, let me know. Okay?"

She nodded her head before taking a pull on her straw. "Thanks, Alex."

CHAPTER
Twenty-Five

Addie

Walking out of the bar, I mentally yelled at myself. I'd just fucking lied to Alex. He asked me point-blank if it had been the first time I had seen David hanging around and I fucking lied to his face.

I didn't lie. I didn't like liars. I thought they were cowards and now, here I was, selling myself out and being one. I don't know why I didn't tell him the truth. He was probably the one person that I *could* tell the truth to but instead...

I shook my head before walking up the steps to my apartment. Sliding the key in the lock, I kicked my shoes off, relieved I had the place to myself. Kelly was out with her friends this weekend and said she wouldn't be back until tomorrow. She was kind of fun to live with, but it was also nice to have some peace and quiet at times.

In the last few weeks, I hadn't seen Charlie much. She wasn't having the easiest pregnancy and I knew she had been struggling to sleep through the night for a full eight hours. She had mentioned the baby using her bladder as a squeeze toy. Naps in the afternoon or early evening were starting to become a part of the normal routine for her.

I grabbed the laptop and loaded it up, deciding to get to work on the invitations I had been designing for her. James and I had decided to throw Charlie and Alex a surprise baby shower. They didn't have a lot of family, and I thought it would be amazing to get all of us together to celebrate.

All of the bar staff, waitresses and cooks from both of their businesses promised to attend. I had even spoken to Charlie's mum, and she was going to come up especially for it and stay until after the baby was born.

James kept teasing me that because he was the uncle, this could maybe boost him up to god-father. He made me laugh. Like there was anyone else to ask to be god-father. He and I had those roles locked down tight already.

I pressed send, emailing all the invites out to everyone with strict instructions not to let Alex or Charlie know that it was happening. We had decided to have it in two months' time. Not too close to the due date but far enough away so that there wouldn't be any early deliveries and Charlie could hopefully enjoy it more.

Closing the laptop, I stood, still feeling tense. I made my way to the kitchen and opened the fridge. I grabbed the bottle of wine that was still in there and poured a large glass. I was still anxious over the truth I had glossed over with Alex and James. I knew it was just a waiting game now. James knew me well enough to know when I was lying or avoiding the truth. He and I had spent a lot of time together over the last year. Alex thought we were hiding a relationship but it had never got to that stage.

After one night out and way too many drinks, we'd had a crazy night together that had slowly turned to several crazy nights. I'd thought he cared for me but I was never sure. We agreed no feelings and that was just how it was.

I wanted to live my life. I wanted to travel the world. I wanted what Alex and Charlie had together one day but not yet. I wanted to live my life first.

My phone beeped with a text message, disturbing my thoughts.

Come to mine tonight. −J

Speak of the devil.

What's in it for me? I have Netflix here ;)

I took a sip of the wine, waiting for his response. This was what our relationship was. Flirts, laughs, dancing, lust and maybe a little bit of passion. Okay, a lot of passion but I wasn't ready to admit to that just yet.

What I want you here for has fuck all to do with Netflix

I laughed loudly at his response, surprised at his cockiness. A lot of people underestimated James, thinking that he was the quiet one, the sweet one. Boy, they were wrong. There was fuck all sweet about James in the bedroom. He was gentle outside of it, but inside, there was nothing he wasn't willing to try.

I guessed that was why we worked so well as friends with benefits. We never expected anything and knew that come morning, we went back to our lives. There were never any expectations and because of that, there was no heartbreak.

I leaned my head back against the cushion, feeling the knots of tension finally begin to unwind. I think telling Alex about David hanging around outside for the last three weeks would be the best decision. Maybe then I would stop feeling so anxious about it and at least I would have two more people on my side and more people to look out for Charlie when I wasn't around.

I reached for my phone, deciding to put James out of his misery. It was seconds too late, though.

The floorboard directly behind me creaked and a hand quickly clamped over my mouth. Seconds later, the sharp prick of a needle went into the side of my neck, draining the fight from my body.

I struggled against the hold on me before I felt the energy begin draining from my arms. The glass of wine toppled, a blood-red stain leaking out over the floor. Kicking my legs was futile, my body beginning to slump, taking the last shred of energy and with it, the last bit of fight.

My eyes closed, succumbing to whatever had been injected into me. I didn't see who was, but it didn't take a rocket scientist to figure it out. There was only one psychotic freak hanging around and it looked like he had finally gone mental.

*W*aking up, it felt like my eyes had been rubbed raw with sandpaper. They felt sore and it was difficult for me to focus. I stared around, cringing at my surroundings. It appeared I was sitting in the middle of a vacant unit. There were oil stains on the floor and a mattress was over against the wall.

"You're awake." David kneeled down in front of me before reaching up and peeling the duct tape that was over my mouth, roughly with no care.

I screamed, glaring up at him. "That hurt, you fucker," I muttered.

"Don't talk like that." He smacked his hand hard across my face, knocking my head to the side. "You're disgusting when you talk like that."

I glared up at him, my eyes widening in shock at him. "Saying naughty words," I mocked, "is disgusting but roping an innocent woman to a chair and kidnapping is okay?" By the end of the question, I was shouting at him.

"Innocent." His lip curled in disgust at me. "I wouldn't call *you* innocent." He turned from me, walking a little away before facing me again. "You stripped for a living, danced around a pole and you sneak off to fuck that James Winters." He smirked at me and it made me want to throw up. "You're far from fucking innocent."

I looked at him in disgust, hating how I felt. I didn't class burlesque dancing as stripping—it wasn't like I was a prostitute—but I was still a little ashamed that that's how I'd made money.

"Me?" I asked. "I'm disgusting?" I trailed my eyes down his limp frame, looking at him like the filth that he was. "You think when Charlie finds out what you've done that you'll be *anything* to her?" I turned my head and spat some blood onto the floor. "You'll be *nothing* to her, David. *Nothing!*"

He glared at me with hatred before his hand shot out and smacked me again. Once. Twice. Three times he smacked me before delivering a punch to my cheekbone. That one was going to leave a mark.

I spat more blood out before looking up at him. "She doesn't need you, David." I shook my head. "I know I'm not perfect, but Charlie is. She looks for the good in people. She would have looked for the good in you but what you did to her..."

"Shut up!" he snapped. He turned away from me.

"You tried to break her but she's better than you. You won't break her."

He shook his head, and I could hear him mutter words to himself under his breath as he began to pace a little.

"She's with Alex now," I continued, "and they are going to be a family," I firmly stated. "Hurting me is only going to break you."

"I said shut up!" he screamed at me before he delivered another punch to my face.

My head slumped back, feeling my eyes begin to close. Before they did, my thoughts went to the message I'd been sending James before David decided to inject shit into my veins. I hoped the message had sent and that James and Alex were on their way to find me.

CHAPTER

Twenty-Six

James

It was a little quiet at the bar. Since Addie had left, a few families had come and gone but the kitchen had been pretty quiet so Alex had gone upstairs an hour previous, leaving me to watch the bar.

My eyes kept going to the clock, cringing when I saw that it wasn't even eight pm yet.

I grabbed my phone, sending a message to Addie.

Come to mine tonight. –J

Addie and I had been spending a lot of time together over the last few months. It had started off as a one-night stand and then one had led to two. A few weeks after that, we were friends with benefits. More benefit than friend.

I didn't know how to be a friend to Addie. I wanted a lot fucking more than just friendliness with her but I knew she wasn't ready for that. She had things she wanted to do first. As I'd watched Alex and Charlie fall in love, I had decided that could be me and Addie. If she wanted to live her life first, I was cool with that. I didn't mind waiting for Addie.

My phone beeped, telling me she had replied.

What's in it for me? I have Netflix here ;)

Sexy little fucking minx. I sent a quick reply back, not in the mood for any games tonight.

What I want you here for has fuck all to do with Netflix

I had expected a woman like Addie to be dominant in the bedroom. I knew she was a burlesque dancer, and I knew that she was confident in her body. I only had to see her outfits to know that she didn't mind being stared at. She was one of the most beautiful women I had ever met. That's why I was shocked as hell when it turned out that I was the dominant one. Addie liked to be bossed around and controlled. It was sexy as hell, and I think that's why we worked. When I thought back to

Addie's ex-sexual partners, I wondered if they'd had the balls to boss her around like that.

Normally, I wasn't bossy in the bedroom, but she brought it out of me. When I was in control of Addie in our sexual adventures, I knew I had her completely. She was sassy as hell, but when it was just her and me, I was able to fool myself into thinking she wanted me as desperately as I craved her.

I put my phone down as a few customers came through the doors. I thought they'd walk back out when I told them that the kitchen was closed for the night, not wanting to disturb Alex's time with Charlie. Instead, they stayed for a few rounds and the night seemed to pick up.

A few hours later, I was closing up the bar. I locked the doors up before heading out of the side exit. Instead of getting in my car to drive home, I walked up the block, grabbing my phone and checking for the hundredth time to see if Addie had sent a response.

She hadn't.

It wasn't the first time she'd blown me off but it *was* the first time she hadn't replied to a flirtatious message. She was a flirt by nature; it was part of her charm. Maybe she was just trying to see how far she could push me before I'd turn up at her door, ready to explode.

I pressed the buzzer, waiting patiently for her voice to come through the speaker. I frowned at her button before pressing it a couple of more times, waiting. It was only just past midnight, and I knew that it was still early for her. She was too used to her burlesque hours. When she'd worked there, she wouldn't have been coming home until gone two am. She was a night owl, and she probably always would be.

I stepped aside, relieved when an older gentleman opened the door. He held it for me before he went down the corridor that led to his apartment. We'd bumped into each other a few times, and he always seemed polite.

I took the stairs two at a time, eager to see her, but freezing when I got to her place, my heart coming to a stop at the sight in front of me. The door was ajar. I checked the frame for signs of a break-in, bending down when I saw Addie's bracelet on the floor in a crack of the tile.

She wore this thing everywhere. It had little charms on it, and she always said it was who she was. I fingered the flat ballet charm dangling from it before I stood up, walking inside. I slipped it into my pocket and rushed over to the sofa. The coffee table was overturned and there was a large red stain on the rug next to an empty wine glass. Her phone was on the floor, and judging by the cracked screen, I assumed it had been thrown in whatever struggle had taken place.

I grabbed the landline's handset from where it was lying discarded on the floor before dialling Alex's mobile number. I waited impatiently for him to pick up, tapping my hand repeatedly against the side of my leg. Just before I went to hang up, his voice echoed down the line.

"Addie?" he croaked down the line.

"It's me," I muttered.

"James?" He sounded a little more awake now. "What is it?"

I heard Charlie in the background, asking what was wrong.

"It's nothing, darling." I heard him lean away from the phone. "Go back to sleep. It's okay." Several moments of silence passed before I heard a door close. "What's wrong?"

"I need you to come to Addie's." I stared at the photo of her and Charlie standing on the windowsill. "Don't bring Charlie," I warned. I put the phone down without saying goodbye.

I spent the moments before Alex arrived checking the apartment. I looked in her bedroom and saw all of her jewellery was still there and her flat-screen television didn't have a scratch on it. After checking her roommate's bedroom, I saw her window was wide open.

I walked back out into the lounge just as Alex came through the door.

"What's the—" He stared past me at the overturned coffee table and the wine stain on the floor.

"It was like this when I got here. The door was ajar and this"—I pulled Addie's bracelet out of my pocket, holding it up for him to see—"was on the floor by the door," I said, pointing at his feet.

"Have you called the police yet?" he asked.

"No." I shook my head needlessly. "I'm still trying to convince myself that this isn't happening."

"Call them," he ordered. "We're going to need them."

I nodded before grabbing the phone. "They are going to want to speak to Charlie."

"I know." He sighed and reached up, rubbing his knuckles against the top of his head. He always did that when he was stressed. "They can do that tomorrow. She needs her rest right now."

After making the phone call, we waited tensely in the kitchen for the police to arrive, trying to ignore how familiar the scene was. Last time this happened, the police had come and taken my brother away, throwing him in prison for several years. He would have been in there longer but because of his good behaviour, he was let out early.

Alex stood up when he heard movement. "In here!" he called. He walked past me, nodding his head for me to follow.

Two police officers—one male and one female— were standing in the lounge. The male officer was staring past us at the mess and the female one was taking a notepad out of her pocket.

"Did you make the call?" she asked, looking at Alex.

"I did," I said. "My name is James Winters and this is my brother Alex."

She wrote a few notes down before she looked back up at us. "In your own words, sir, can you explain what happened tonight?"

"I, uh, I finished work just before midnight. I work for my brother at the bar just down the street," I said, pointing my fingers at the open doorway behind her.

"Alex's bar, right?" she asked, confirming with us.

"That's right." I nodded my head. "Addie and I are friends, and I came here to check on her." I could feel Alex staring at me. "We had been texting each other earlier in the night and she hadn't text me back for a couple of hours."

"When did you see her last?" she asked.

"She came by the bar," James inserted. "She had a coke at the bar and then she went home around seven-ish. I worked the rest of my shift and after locking up and came this way to check on her. I left my car outside the bar..."

The police officer stared past us before she subtly nodded her head. "Is there anything else?" she asked.

I looked at Alex, waiting for his input. He just stared at the officer, making me want to smack him.

"Alex's girlfriend, Charlotte Chase, used to live here."

She cocked an eyebrow at me at my words.

"Charlie moved out a while ago and moved in with my brother."

Alex sighed before putting his hands in his pockets. "My girlfriend has had a few problems from an ex-partner of hers."

"What's the name?" the male officer behind us asked.

"David Smith," Alex answered. "You're probably going to want to check the name out."

She nodded before she turned away from us, walking to the door and speaking into the walkie-talkie clipped to her collar. She came back a few minutes later before she walked up to Alex.

"We are going to need to speak to Miss Chase," she said to Alex.

"She's sleeping," he said. "She's pregnant and hasn't been very well lately."

She nodded before turning away and speaking into her walkie-talkie. "Thank you both for your co-operation." She put her notepad back in her pocket. "If you can both go home and we will be in touch in the morning."

"But what about Addie?" I asked. Were they fucking high? A young woman goes missing and they thought that they could just send us home for the night? They needed to be out there looking for her!

"James." Alex placed his hand on my shoulder and turned me to face him. "Let's go."

I opened my mouth to say something, but before I could, he was shaking his head.

"We need to let them conduct their investigation." He widened his eyes at me, and I knew that he was trying to keep me calm. "You'll stay with me tonight, and they can come to the bar in the morning and take Charlie's statement there."

The police officer nodded her head before stepping aside and allowing us to walk past her to the door.

I stopped when I got there, remembering what was in my pocket.

"Oh, I, uh, I found this when I got here. It's Addie's bracelet." I dropped it into her hand. "I'm sorry. I probably shouldn't have picked it up."

"Thank you." She gave me a polite smile, remaining professional before turning away and walking to face her partner.

"Come on, little brother." Alex grabbed my shoulder and gently steered me to the door. "Let's go and hopefully tomorrow they will have some information.

We exited the apartment building, and as we walked down the block towards Alex's home, I could feel dread taking up residence in my chest. She had to be okay. I don't know what I was going to do if she wasn't okay.

"What are we going to do?" I asked as we approached the bar. "What are we going to do if the police don't find anything?"

He sighed, unlocking the door and opening it. He nodded his head for me to go in first before he followed behind.

"If they don't find anything," he said, answering my question before he turned and locked the doors. "You and I will start our own investigation."

"What about Charlie?" I asked. "She's not going to take this well."

"I'll tell her in the morning. I don't want to disturb whatever rest she's managed to get tonight." He walked past me, leading the way to the staircase. "You can stay on the sofa and then in the morning..."

He froze as he went through the door and I saw his shoulders slump. He stepped aside and held the door open for me to come in before he closed the door.

Charlie was sitting on the sofa, wrapped in a blanket. "What's wrong?" she whispered. She looked past Alex at me before looking back to him. She rested her hand on her large bump before she asked again more firmly. "Alex, what's wrong?" Her voice wavered and I knew right then that Charlie was going to go to pieces when she found out about Addie.

CHAPTER

Twenty-Seven

Alex

I stared at her, hating that it fell to me now to break her heart. I always promised myself that I would never be the one to break her and now, because of that arsehole, I would have to break my word.

She stood as I walked to her, and I wrapped my arm around her shoulders pulling her into my chest before I kissed her forehead.

"Let's go into the bedroom," I whispered. I wanted to give her privacy when I shattered her world. "We can talk in there." I turned back to James. "Call Addie's room-mate. Tell her what's going on."

Charlie always came across as a private person. I

think the only time I had seen her cry was when we heard the heartbeat of our child for the first time.

She took my hand and followed me to our bedroom. I pulled her down next to me before cradling her face in my hands.

"You're scaring me," she whispered. Her eyes trailed to the gap in the open doorway. "James looks…"

"James," I started, "went to see Addie tonight." I twirled her daisy ring a little, trying to prolong what I was about to say next. "She wasn't there."

"What do you mean?" she whispered.

"She was gone." Her eyes widened at my words, but I quickly continued. "The coffee table was overturned and she…" I shook my head, feeling tongue-tied. "Her wine glass was spilled over on the rug and her mobile phone was on the floor with a cracked screen."

"No," she whispered. Her eyes filled before she shook her head. "No!" She sobbed before her shoulders began shaking.

I pulled her into me, hating the way that my chest hurt with every hiccup and sob that came from her small body.

"I'm sorry, baby." I slid my arm beneath her knees and picked her up, lifting her across my lap. I rocked her from side to side, trying to ease her grief with my touch. I could feel the wetness from her tears soaking into my shirt, and I wanted to smash my fist into David's face for every one of them that fell. I moved us up the bed a little, keeping my grip on her, being careful not to jostle her too much. I laid us down, holding her hand over my heart. After a while, her tears slowly stopped before she lifted her head.

"Did you call the police?" she rasped. Her eyes were swollen from the waterfall of tears that had dripped down her cheeks.

"We did, darling. We left them at Addie's apartment." I rubbed my hand up and down her arm. "They are going to call here in the morning to speak to you. I told them about David."

"Do you think it was him?" she asked. She rested her chin on my chest, looking up at me.

"I hope not but..." I blew out a breath. "I don't really know who else it could be that would want to hurt her."

She nodded at my words, not arguing.

"I would kill him if he ever took you away from me like that." I meant it. It wasn't a threat or a promise: it was a fucking vow. I would happily serve time in prison again if he ever laid a hand on my girl. I placed my hand on her bump, feeling the baby kick.

"Don't say that," she whispered. Her lower lip wobbled. "I hate to think of you locked up. It breaks my heart, Alex."

"I know, baby." I dipped my head and kissed her lips softly before pulling back. "I mean it, though. I love you too damn fucking much to ever let that bastard walk if he hurt you."

A moment of silence passed before she spoke again.

"Do you think she's okay?" she whispered. "Do you think he's hurting her?"

I stared at her trusting face, wanting to lie to her to spare her feelings. I couldn't lie to her any more than she could lie to me, though.

"I think." I hesitated, trying to choose my words. "I think Addie is strong. She's tough, and I think she will do whatever it takes to get home to us." I stroked my fingers along her cheekbone. "To you."

She nodded her head before she laid her head back down on my chest, tightening her arm around my waist.

We both lay there in the darkness, both of our thoughts lost to wherever Addie was.

I prayed that night—not for the first time—for the strength that would be needed to get through the rest of this ordeal. I hoped like hell that Addie would come home to us, but I was terrified about what state we would find her in—scared how far that fucker would push it. If this didn't work out, if we lost Addie, I would lose the three most important people in my world: my brother, my girl and the little life growing inside of her.

There was no way in fucking hell, I was going to let that happen.

*S*itting down in the bar the next morning, I watched Charlie as she fidgeted with the hem of her jumper. It was the third time she had pulled it down over her thighs.

"I wish you had eaten something this morning." I took her hand, squeezing it gently.

"I wasn't hungry." She shook her head before looking at James, watching him pace back and forth by the door to the kitchen. "Did he sleep last night?" she asked, worrying.

He looked like he hadn't had a wink of sleep last night, and he was way too wired from coffee.

"James," I called. "Come and sit with us." I nodded my head to Charlie, widening my eyes at him, trying to hint at him to ease up a little.

He nodded before coming over and taking a seat next to Charlie.

"Did you sleep last night?" she asked him.

"Yes." He nodded his head, giving her a small smile. "I've just had too much coffee."

"Right," she muttered. She knew he was lying to her, but she didn't call him out on it. She reached over and placed her hand over his, giving it a squeeze before her attention was taken by the main doors opening. We all straightened up when the same set of police officers walked in from last night. They weren't alone, though. An older male in a grey suit walked in with them. He looked to be in his early fifties and had a polite smile on his face.

"Hello. I'm Detective Michaels, and I'm lead investigator on this case." He held his hand out to James and me, shaking our hands and took a seat opposite us. He gave a polite smile to Charlie before holding his hand out across the table to her. "You must be Charlotte Chase."

"Yes," she croaked. She gave a small smile, shaking his hand. "Do you have any new information?" she asked, desperation leaking into her tone.

"I'm afraid not." He placed his arms on the table before linking his fingers. "I am here to ask some follow-up questions linking to Mr. Winters' statement that he gave my officers last night."

"About what?" I asked.

"About Mr. David Smith." He looked at Charlie. "I understand he is an ex-partner of yours, Miss Chase."

"Yes." She nodded her head. "We separated over a year ago. It was an amicable split at the time."

"At the time," he said, repeating her words. "And that has changed over the last year?" She didn't have a chance to answer before he was continuing with his next question. "Before you answer that, may I ask, what caused the separation?"

"I went to visit him in the office as he was working late one evening." She fidgeted, pulling on the ends of her sleeves. "I walked into his office and he was..." She stopped, clearing her throat before continuing. "He was screwing his receptionist."

"I see." He had a good poker face. "Were you and he living together at the time?"

"No." She shook her head exaggeratedly. "Before I moved in with Alex, I had been living with Addie for three years. She's my best friend, sir." She was getting choked up, and I knew it wasn't going to take long before she would break.

"I see. So, when do you think it was that it went from an amicable split to more than that?" He had a polite expression on his face, but I wasn't appreciative of the type of questions he was asking. He was putting pressure on her and I didn't fucking like it.

"I, uh, I noticed him hanging outside my building during his lunch a couple of times a week a few months after we separated. I didn't think much of it because his office was only a block away. We always used to meet up at a sandwich shop opposite my building for lunch when we could."

"I see." He nodded for her to continue.

"It began happening more often and that's when I began to think that there was a problem."

"Did his behaviour start getting more erratic?" he asked. "Did you ever consider approaching him about his behaviour?"

"No," she answered. She reached over and placed her hand on top of mine on the table, smiling at me when I squeezed her fingers. "I ignored it. I didn't have anything I thought needed saying since our break-up." She shrugged her shoulders. "He followed me home a few times after that, and I saw him sitting on the bench opposite the apartment building a few times."

"Has Mr. Smith ever approached you, Mr. Winters?" he asked, directing his question to me.

"Yes." I nodded my head. "When Charlie and I began dating, he came into the bar and began shouting about our relationship." I could feel my temper rising. "It was around that time that Charlie had a break-in to her apartment and I changed the locks for her."

"A break-in?" He looked at Charlie sharply. "Was that reported?" He had an edge to his tone now.

"No." She shook her head. "I was taking a shower and I heard a noise. When I turned, the bathroom door and the door to the apartment was wide open." She looked at me before turning back to face the detective. "The next day, he came to the apartment shouting because Alex was there. They had a little fight and then David left." Her fingers began rubbing small circles in her bump. "The next day we went to the station to report his behaviour."

The detective nodded his head, holding his hand up to halt her. "I've seen the case report," he answered. "I understand he made an assault charge against you, Mr. Winters and then, you, yourself, made a formal complaint, Miss Chase."

"Has that helped at all?" Charlie asked.

"It has, yes." He nodded his head. "Thank you for your time, Miss Chase."

She stood, still holding my hand before stopping when the detective continued to talk.

"If you can excuse us, Miss Chase. I would like a word with you both," he said, gesturing to me and James. "I just have a few follow-up questions on the statements that were given last night."

She nodded before bending down and kissed my cheek. "I'll just go upstairs and have a lie-down, if that's okay."

"Of course." I brought the back of her hand up to my lips, kissing the soft skin there. "I'll be up when I'm done."

She nodded her head before walking behind the bar, leaving us to it.

"James. If you can tell me in your own words what happened last night from the last time that you physically saw and spoke with the victim."

James flinched.

Victim. It sounded so fucking cold and calculating. Like Addie wasn't a person. Like she was just a body in an investigation.

CHAPTER
Twenty-Eight

Charlie

I went up to Alex's apartment, taking a seat on the sofa. I was sure the day would come where I'd be comfortable calling it *our* apartment instead of his.

I looked at the photograph of Addie and me that was sitting on the shelf above the fireplace. We were downstairs in the corner booth. There were cocktails on the table and we both had our arms wrapped around each other with huge grins on both of our faces. I still felt numb over this situation. This couldn't be happening.

When I'd first met David, he had been so kind and caring. When we'd dated, he had sometimes been outspoken about my outfits or my plans, but kidnapping a woman was a huge leap from the man that I had first met. When the detective had been asking me questions downstairs, I'd known he had no fresh leads. I knew that with every question he asked me—I knew it deep in my bones—that he had no clue where to start looking for Addie and David. I had watched more than enough crime investigation documentaries with Addie. I knew they would have checked David's home by now. I also knew that it was only a matter of time before he either made contact or took it past the point of no return.

I was shaken out of my dark thoughts when my phone began ringing. I looked at the screen and saw it was a withheld number. I normally didn't answer telephone numbers that I didn't know. Withheld or private numbers usually went straight to the voicemail.

Today was different, though.

"Hello."

Silence greeted me.

"Hello," I said louder. I pulled the phone from my ear, looking at the screen to see if the call was still connected. It was. The call duration was still ticking the seconds away.

"David?" I asked, taking a stab in the dark. "David? Is that you?"

"It's me." He sounded so cold and dismissive.

"David, what have you done?" I asked. "Where's Addie?"

"She's here. She's alive," he answered. "I need to

see you." My hand tensed on my bump, guarding the life growing inside of me. "I won't hurt you," he continued. "I won't hurt you, I promise. I just need to see you."

My thoughts went straight to the boys downstairs, but before I could get up, his voice spoke again, stopping me.

"Don't tell anyone," he threatened. "If you dare, I won't hesitate to put a bullet in her head." A moment of silence passed before he spoke again. "I won't hurt you. I just want to see you," he said, sounding a little calmer now. "Go downstairs. There's a taxi waiting for you. Get into it and leave your phone behind." The sound of the call hanging up came through the line.

I put my hand over my mouth, trying to contain the sobs. I placed my other hand over my belly, torn about what to do. Did I risk everything I have or did I let Addie suffer the consequences? Did I put my friend first or my baby?

I looked down at my phone, hesitating before standing up. I grabbed my phone and walked to the door, typing a message to Alex. I didn't hit send until I was at the bottom of the staircase. I placed the phone on the bottom step, hit send and disappeared out of the side door.

I believed in Alex. I believed he would come for me. I knew he had CCTV surveillance installed, and I believed he would work with the police. All that they had to do was check the taxi number and follow it.

Alex wouldn't let me down. He hadn't yet, and I knew that he never would.

———

*a*s I exited the bar, there was a black cab taxi idling at the kerb. I hopped in, and the driver immediately pulled away. I looked through the back window, relieved when I saw Alex come running out the side door with James and the detective chasing behind him. As we disappeared out of view, I sent a prayer to God, asking for his protection for all of my loved ones today. If he got us through this, I would be forever grateful.

I gazed around, trying to pick up some signs on where he was taking me. He took a lot of the back roads, and I knew that wherever David was keeping Addie, it was somewhere in the direction of the industrial parks near the outside of the city. I looked out the back and side windows, trying to catch a glimpse of James's vehicle. I was terrible at recognising car makes. There was no way that I could pick it out of the traffic around us.

Around twenty minutes later, the car came to a stop. I stared at the driver in a panic, realising that I didn't have my purse with me.

"There you go." He gave me a polite smile in the rear-view mirror. "Your friend already paid the fare when he called to hire us." His eyes narrowed at me, probably wondering why I wasn't moving.

I caught on, nodding my head before climbing out. I looked around, trying to stay calm when the taxi pulled away, leaving me behind. I looked around the industrial estate. It seemed deserted. There were several units with their shutters pulled down, except for the one in front of me. The shutters were up and the uPVC door was wide open.

I took a deep breath before straightening my shoulders and walked inside, making sure to remain as quiet as possible, not wanting to draw any attention to myself. If I could get Addie out and away from here, I would be happy.

The ground floor was deserted. There were a few oil stains on the floor but there didn't seem to be anyone in sight. I walked quietly towards the back of the unit where I saw a metal staircase leading up to another floor. I took the steps slowly, one at a time, craning my neck to try and see the landing above me. I tensed with anxiety with every step I took and then I saw her. I ran up the last few steps, grabbing the railing, using it to launch myself higher.

"Addie!" I lifted her head, hating the way it was slumped. She had duct tape across her mouth and her arms and legs were roped to the legs and back of the chair. She had bruises on her arms and a cut across her eyebrow with dried blood down the side of her face. "Addie!" I shook her forcefully, needing her awake.

Looking around, I wondered where the hell David was. There was no way he brought me all the way out here for me to just walk back out with Addie without any confrontation.

I shook her again before smacking her hard across the face, needing to shock some life back into her.

Her head shot to the side before she lifted it.

I sighed in relief when her eyes met mine. I grabbed the edge of the tape and ripped it off, not having the time for gentleness.

"Ow, you bitch!" She rubbed her lips together, attempting to ease the soreness. "That slap hurt."

I couldn't contain the chuckle that came from me.

"I'm sorry. Let me get these things off." I grabbed the knots binding her arms together, tugging for several moments and starting to panic when they wouldn't undo. I finally loosened them enough for her to slip her cut wrists through before she helped me untie the knots on her legs. I grabbed her arm and slung it over my shoulders before I began pulling her towards the staircase.

"Where is he?" I muttered, my eyes darting around to spy him.

"I don't know." She held her side, gasping in pain. "He's a fucking psycho."

I rolled my eyes at her, feeling relief course through me when I saw that we were almost at the staircase. Before we could descend them, however, the door at the top of the stairs opened and David walked out, pointing a gun in our direction.

"David," I whispered. I looked at the gun terrified.

"Look at you!" He gazed down at my bump with disgust. "Didn't take you long did it?"

I placed my hands on my bump protectively. It was making my skin crawl the way that he was looking at me.

"David, she needs medical attention." Her hair was matted with blood and I really didn't like the way that she was holding her side. Addie had a high pain threshold and for her to be gasping, I knew that it had to be bad.

"She can go," he said. "You can stay."

"No fucking way!" Addie fired back. "Charlie comes with me."

"What did I say about your mouth?" he shouted, waving the gun back in her direction.

"It's okay, Addie." I unwrapped my arm from around her shoulders before resting my hand on the bottom of her back. "It's okay. You go." I could sense her looking at me in shock from the corner of my eye. "Go. I will stay here with David." I made sure to keep my tone calm and low, not wanting to frighten anyone.

"Are you fucking crazy?" she whispered. It was too low for David to hear, which I was thankful for.

"Go," I said, dismissing her. "David won't hurt me." I kept repeating it to myself, so that maybe I would believe it.

David gave me a small smile at my response, and I knew the man I'd once cared for was gone already. It broke my heart that he had fully checked out on reality, but the life of my child came before him. He had made his decision to hurt Addie, and now it was up to me to do whatever it took to get myself and my child out of this room and back to Alex.

Addie nodded her head at me before she began walking slowly past him.

I stared at her back, silently urging her to get the fuck out of dodge before all hell broke loose. I could feel my anxiety building as she cautiously approached the top of the staircase. Before she could take a step down, she turned at the last second and grabbed him. She threw her whole body into it and I could see what she was thinking. My crazy best friend was planning to throw David down the metal staircase.

He dropped the gun at her actions, frightening everyone when a shot rang out, a bullet piercing the concrete wall. He threw Addie backward, slamming her into the wall behind them at the top of the staircase.

I leaped forward, grabbing the gun, trying to gain the upper hand. Before I could threaten David and force him to let Addie go, they both lurched to the side. I froze and watched in slow motion as they both went tumbling down the staircase.

"Addie!" I screamed as I ran towards them. I reached out to grab her hand but I was too late.

They both went down, not stopping until they were near the bottom.

I quickly took the steps. I tried so hard not to focus on how still and quiet Addie was. She wasn't moving. I looked at David and saw the muscles of his back moving, signifying he was breathing as he lay face down on the concrete floor.

I put the gun down before I turned to Addie, placing my hand on her back, needing to check she was okay. She had to be knocked out. Maybe she hit her head on the metal railing.

David groaned before he rolled over. He reached for the railing and used it as leverage to pull himself up. "Fucking bitch!" he muttered.

I grabbed the handgun. I hadn't been prepared to take a life, but he had already hurt my best friend. If he tried to hurt my baby, damn right I was going to defend it by taking his.

He stood up, wobbling. He lifted his hand, resting it against his forehead before pulling it back. His head was bleeding profusely and he looked like he was limping a little.

"I'm really sorry about this, baby." He reached

behind him and pulled a gun from his waistband. "I really am." He stared at me with sorrow, and I knew that somewhere inside, he *was* sorry. It was too late for that, though. "I tried to have you, but you just wouldn't listen." He waved the gun at me, and I could see his anger beginning to take over.

He cocked it aiming it at my head, but then slowly lowered it and aimed it at my bump.

I tensed.

"I wanted everything with you but I…" He shook his head. "I can't live with this."

I didn't hesitate. I lifted my hand with the gun and aimed it at him. I pulled the trigger, protecting the life inside of me. I froze when the gun didn't fire.

David smirked at me before he took a step closer. He slowly raised the gun and aimed it at my head again. "I'll see you in the next life, baby girl."

I closed my eyes, feeling the tears travel down my cheeks. Memories flashed through my mind: Addie, James, Alex.

Alex, Alex, Alex…

I hoped he would go on. I hoped that he would continue to live.

I waited for the gun to fire, but he just stood there, staring at me. I jumped in shock, surprised when men infiltrated the warehouse. Eight to ten police officers swarmed the office, holding flashlights. They had taser guns strapped to their hips. I watched in stunned silence as the detective from this morning walked through the gap and address David.

"Mr. Smith, I need you to lower the gun." He put his hand up, stopping Alex from walking too close to the front. I cried when I saw him, wanting nothing more than to be wrapped in his arms.

"I didn't hurt her," David called. He looked at me. "I'll be seeing you, Charlie." He lifted his hand and held the gun to the side of his head. He didn't hesitate. He pulled the trigger, blowing his brains all over the wall before his body slumped to the ground.

I screamed, shocked to the core.

Seconds later, Alex was pushing his way through the crowd, pulling my shaking body up and into his arms.

"It's okay, darling. I've got you." He tightened his arms around my body and pulled me further away. "It's okay. It's okay."

CHAPTER
Twenty-Nine

Alex

The second his body slumped, I ran forward, pushing my way through. I leaned down and pulled her shaking body up and into my arms. "It's okay, darling. I've got you." I reached around and tightened my arms around her body, pulling her away from where David and Addie were lying. "It's okay. It's okay."

I looked at Addie, hating how still she was. She wasn't moving. It didn't even look like she was breathing. Paramedics came running through the door with a stretcher loaded down with first aid equipment.

"I need to get you out of here." I turned her body to face the exit and began walking her away.

"I need to see Addie," she whispered, craning her neck. "I need to be with her."

"We need to give them room to work on her." I moved her to the door, not wanting her to be here to see this.

As we went through the doorway, another ambulance came speeding into the estate before coming to a stop. A paramedic jumped out of the driver's side and ran around to the back of the truck. They both grabbed a bag each and went running past us.

I sat Charlie down on the wall outside and knelt down in front of her. I squeezed her hands, unable to take my eyes off her.

"She wasn't moving." Tears streamed down her face. Her lower lip wobbled before she tightened her fingers on mine. "They both went toppling down the stairs and she wasn't moving." She choked on a sob and it fucking broke me.

Every tear. Every sob. Every tremor that went through her body... I took it all and it broke me inside.

"I'm sorry about David, darling." I reached up and placed my hand on her bump. Relief coursed through me when I felt a kick. "I want to take you and have you checked over by a paramedic."

She nodded at my words. Before she could say anything, her eyes shot past me.

I stood, squeezing her hand before turning to face the detective. "How is she?" I asked.

The detective stared at me before looking down at Charlie. He placed his hands in his pockets before his shoulders slumped.

"I am very sorry, Miss Chase. I'm afraid Miss Michaels banged her head a little too hard coming down the steps and she…"

"No!" Charlie clapped her hand over her mouth. "NO! Please no!"

"I am very sorry." He dipped his head before he walked to a police car.

I bent down, pulling her into my arms and crushed her against me. Her sobs were painful, and I knew that this news was devastating her. This was *not* how today was supposed to end. Today should have ended with David being arrested and out of our lives.

Instead, Charlie's whole life had just turned upside down.

---

*W*aiting outside for a few moments, Charlie had been staring at the wall with tears streaming down her face. She looked like a shattered doll. I stood when a paramedic came over and nodded his head towards the ambulance.

"Darling." I bent down, pushing my body into her line of sight. "Darling," I said louder.

She gazed up at me. She looked so lost.

"I would like you to be checked over by a paramedic."

She nodded, letting me guide her up. Charlie had always been so delicate, but right now she was fragile. One false move and she would break, and I was terrified more than ever that I wouldn't be able to put her back together.

The paramedic gestured for her to take a seat on the stretcher before they lifted her up and wheeled her into the ambulance.

"Don't leave me!" she shouted, reaching her hand out for me.

I quickly hopped up, taking her hand in mine. "Is there a problem?" I asked, wondering why the fuck they were strapping her down.

"They have better equipment at the hospital, sir." He looked down at Charlie, giving her a polite smile. "Mummy has been under a bit of stress today, so I think giving her a scan to check on what's going on inside would be the best course of action."

"Okay." I looked out the doors, my eyes trailing to the police officers. I closed my eyes, hating the sight that would be forever burned into my mind: two body bags being wheeled out of the unit that almost cost me my own world.

The other paramedic slammed the back doors closed before he went around to the front.

I brought Charlie's hand up to my lips, kissing the

back of her hand. I held it against my lips a little longer than normal before letting go. "I love you," I whispered.

"I love you." Her eyes filled with tears. She closed them, causing them to leak out of the corners before she opened them again as the ambulance began to pull away. "What about James?" she whispered.

I fell in love with her all over again when she asked that. Even when her world was falling apart, she still thought of other people.

The sounds of sirens sped past us, and I hoped that they were on their way to tell James. I hated that I couldn't be with him when they told him, but right now, Charlie needed me with her. Charlie and our baby needed me. I knew James would understand that.

"First we get you checked out, darling." I rubbed her upper thigh, trying not to crowd the paramedic as he placed a blood pressure cuff around her upper arm. "We will see James when we get home." I looked at the paramedic. "Will she be able to come home tonight?"

He shook his head at me regretfully.

"She will likely be kept in for observation, to be on the safe side."

I nodded, relieved that her eyes were closed. I hoped she wasn't listening but knowing her, she was just resting.

e had been at the hospital for over an hour and were still waiting to speak to a doctor. They had given her a scan as soon as she'd arrived. She'd burst into tears when she'd heard the heartbeat, and I was thankful to hear it too. We couldn't lose our baby—it would kills us both—but also, I was terrified that I wasn't enough. That after the effects of today, after the loss of her best friend... I was scared I wouldn't be enough to pull her forward. That maybe I wouldn't be enough for her to go on.

This baby, though... She would never let her baby down. She would live for her baby.

"Come on," I muttered.

She turned her head from where it was resting on the pillow of the hospital bed to look at me. "You are going to need to learn some patience." She looked down at her bump before she gently rubbed her palms over it. "I think we both are."

I took a seat in the chair next to her bed. "I should have been there," I muttered.

"Alex, don't." More tears leaked out of her eyes. "He had Addie. I had to go."

"I wish I could have protected her," I whispered. "Protected you both."

"She protected me. I told her to go and that I would stay." A sad smile crossed her face. "I should have known that she wouldn't leave me."

"She saved you." I was in awe of Addie once again. It was clear to me that her last actions on this earth were ones of courage. She had saved two lives and given her own. I couldn't stop my own eyes from filling as tears slowly trickled down my face.

"She saved both of us." She reached for my hand, entwining our fingers. "Oh, Alex."

I brought her hand to my mouth, pressing a kiss there before resting it and mine on the mattress between us. "She's a hero."

"She is," she whispered. She reached up and wiped the wetness from her cheeks. "She's my hero."

*W*e weren't kept waiting much longer until a doctor finally came in. He looked to be mid-forties and had a pair of spectacles hanging low on the bridge of his nose.

"Miss Chase. I am sorry to keep you waiting." He gave us both a polite smile. "I am happy to report that everything looks okay and the baby does *not* appear to be under any undue strain."

"So I can go home?" she asked.

"I am afraid not." He shook his head and signed something on the bottom of the chart. "I would like to keep you in tonight, just for observation." He looked at me before looking back at Charlie. "You went through a terrible ordeal today, and I would just like to make sure that there are no problems before I send you home. It's not just the baby to look after. The mother's mental health is just as important."

"I don't like hospitals," she muttered.

"I understand that, but just one night." He patted her arm and looked at me. "You can pick her up in the morning and take her home then."

"I can't stay with her?" I asked.

"I'm afraid not." He shook his head and slid his pen back in the chest pocket of his white, lab coat. "We'll take good care of her, I promise." He walked away leaving us alone.

It was almost eight pm before I was being kicked out.

"You should go," Charlie said. "James needs you, too." She cushioned her head back against the pillow. "I'll be okay. I have my scratchy gown on. I'll go to sleep when you go."

I stared at her for a moment before I slowly nodded my head. I stood up and bent down, kissing her forehead. "I'll be here in the morning." I looked down at her, hating how red and puffy her eyes looked. "If there's a problem..." I placed her mobile phone on the bedside cabinet. "Call me. Okay?"

She stared at me for a moment before she slowly nodded her head. She tilted it, offering her lips to me in a kiss. She grabbed my t-shirt and pulled my mouth down to hers, kissing me softly before letting me go. "Hurry back to me," she whispered.

I placed my hand on her bump for a moment as I left her bedside, walking to the door.

I left the hospital, feeling the weight of the world on my shoulders. I felt like the events of the night were sitting on my chest, and I knew that our lives were never going to be the same. I used to think that the day I killed my father for beating my mother up was the worst day of my life—that it could only get better from there.

I'd been so fucking wrong.

That day had had nothing on today. Today, the world ended for two of the most special people in my life, and I knew it would fall to me to keep it turning. I *had* to keep it turning.

I stood outside the bar, staring up at the street at Addie's apartment building. Police were parked outside, and I assumed they were still looking for evidence. I stared up to my apartment above the bar and saw that the lights were on. I unlocked the side door and walked inside, locking back up before going upstairs. I took a deep breath at the door before walking inside.

James looked up at me from where he was sitting on the sofa. His cheeks were red and his eyes were swollen. There was a half-empty bottle of scotch on the coffee table in front of him.

I shut the door and walked towards him.

He got up, leaning his hand on the sofa to help stabilise him.

"Hey, little brother." I held my arms out, offering him support in the only way that I knew how.

"Hey, man," he croaked out.

I crushed him into a tight hug before I felt his shoulders begin to shake.

He turned his head into my neck, sobbing, the wetness from his tears soaking into my t-shirt.

"Let it out, man." I patted the back of his head, determined not to break. I would be his pillar of strength like he had always been for me. "I'm here. Let it all out."

CHAPTER

Thirty

Alex

Two months later

It had been two months since our world had changed. Two months since our own walking version of sunshine had gone and left our lives a little bit darker.

I had spent the last month watching Charlie, and I could see that with every day, I was losing her. Gone were the smiles. Gone was the excitement when she would make a new treat. When she wasn't making sweets for the shop, she was either reading a book or staring at the wall.

The ring I had bought for her was sitting in my sock drawer. The future I had once pictured for us was now gone. The woman I was having a child with was numb and had become lost to her nightmares. I tried to reach her every day. It worked occasionally but for the most part, she was lost to me.

"How is Charlie doing?" James asked, looking past me at the stairs to the apartment.

"She's okay," I responded automatically. "She's resting." The lie came so easily from my mouth.

He stared at me for a moment before he nodded his head. He didn't believe me. He knew when I was lying, but I didn't really know what else to say.

"How are you?" I asked.

"Meh." He shrugged his shoulders. "I have my days —days where I can't function without looking at her photograph; days where I can smell her perfume all around me. Nights are sometimes the worst."

"You loved her," I stated.

"No." He reached for a glass, cleaning it before placing it on the shelf behind him.

"Maybe. I was getting there; I can't lie about that." He blew out a breath. "But she never loved me. *We*," he said, emphasising the word, "never let it get that far."

"You wanted to, though. Didn't you?" I asked bluntly.

"I did. She was beautiful and we understood each other but she…" A small smile graced his face, and I knew his thoughts were lost in a memory with Addie. "Addie wanted to live and experience the world. She never wanted to be tied down. She was too much of a free spirit for that."

I nodded, not really knowing what else to say.

"I didn't love Addie the way that you and Charlie love each other." He leaned his elbow on the bar, resting his weight on it before he spoke again. "So, how is Charlie?" he asked in a firm tone.

I placed a box of crisps down on the floor beneath the counter before I walked away. I grabbed a stool opposite him from the customer's side of the bar. "She's not good, man. Sometimes she's with me but most of the time…" I could feel my voice shaking. "The only time she's my Charlie again is when we talk about the baby."

"Do you still have the ring?" he asked.

"Yes." I picked a drink mat up and began ripping the corners of it apart. "I've decided to take it to a pawn shop later."

"Are you guys…" He looked at me in shock before he continued. "Are you going to end things?"

"No!" I snapped. I took a breath, attempting to calm my nerves a little. "It's just not the time." I hated the sorrow I could see reflected back at me. "I'm getting to the point where I feel like David won, James." I tossed the mat back on the bar before sliding off my stool. "David won this game." I walked past the bar and took the steps two at a time. I had gotten into the obsessive habit of checking on her every hour.

Since that fateful day, I'd had the same recurring dream. I dreamt that I would arrive to find Charlie and

Addie, *both* dead on the floor of the unit with a knife protruding from Charlie's pregnant stomach. The image always left me feeling cold, and I was lucky to get a few hours of sleep a night. The rest of my night would be spent watching her sleep.

Last week, James and I had decorated the nursery. We had cleared a room I'd been using to hold items for the bar downstairs and had decorated it. It was Dumbo-themed because it had been Charlie's favourite film as a little girl and we felt it matched for either a boy or a girl.

I walked towards it and froze at the door when I heard movement inside. I looked through the gap of the door and saw Charlie. It was the first time I had seen her in there. I heard her sniffling and it broke my fucking heart. It broke me because she always hid her tears from me. If I came into the room, she'd stop crying. If it was the middle of the night and she knew I was awake, she'd go to the bathroom. I hated that she was so afraid to cry in front of me.

I watched as she walked to the rocking chair her mother had bought for us. It was an oak chair with a high back. It was beautiful and I knew that Charlie or I were going to spend many evenings there rocking our child.

"Hi baby," she whispered.

I tensed, thinking that she'd seen me but before I could move, she began talking again.

"I thought it was time that we had a chat."

I leaned my head back against the wall, not wanting to invade on this moment between mother and child but still needing to be here to hear it.

"I haven't been a very good mummy lately."

I heard movement and imagined her rubbing her hands over her stomach.

"This is your nursery. Your daddy and uncle James decorated it for you." A pause. "They can't wait to meet you. Especially your daddy."

I looked across the room and saw a picture of Addie and Charlie sitting on a shelf. They looked so happy.

"Your auntie Addie…" She paused before a small sob left her. "Your auntie Addie isn't here. She was going to spoil you rotten but she…" She took a deep breath before blowing it out. "She's not here, and I really don't know how to do any of this without her."

I hated the sting of rejection I felt at her words. I felt like I had lost her before but listening to her talk like that, I realised that for the first time, she herself sounded lost.

I stood and quietly walked out of the apartment, leaving her alone. I went back downstairs and walked past James, ignoring the look on his face.

"Let me borrow your car." I held my hand up and waited for him to toss the keys to me.

"Where are you going?" James called as he threw the keys at me.

"Out," I replied.

I wasn't in the mood to explain myself any further. James knew me well enough to know when there was something seriously wrong and to leave me to it. The way I was feeling right now, time away from here was the best thing for me. I needed to get away from here to calm myself down. If I stayed, I'd end up losing my temper and would probably end up shouting at the one person that I had come to be unable to live without.

I walked outside, and after unlocking the car, I climbed inside and drove away from the building. I'd always known that she had the power to break me, but I'd never imagined that it would be like this. I never imagined it would be happening during what should have been the happiest time of our lives. In a perfect world, she should have a ring on her finger and we should have been getting ready to merge our lives together. Instead, I was losing her and I had no fucking clue how to fix this.

*a*fter stopping off at a shop to pick up some flowers, I continued driving for another hour until I was arriving at Highgate Cemetery. We had laid Addie to rest there several weeks ago. A beautiful spot had been picked out for her right beneath an oak tree.

"Hi, Adds." I placed the roses on the floor for her before I kneeled down and settled next to her grave. I stared at the dates on her gravestone and it made me angry. She was too damn fucking young to be laying here.

"I'm sorry that we haven't been by." I stared at the lillies lying next to the roses, knowing it was James who had brought them. "Things have been a little tough." I blew out an agitated breath before continuing. "I think I'm losing her, Addie." My fists tensed in my lap, and I hated it. "If you were here, I know you'd be able to fix this. I don't know what I need to do here." I looked across the greenery. It was so quiet here and I hoped that she was resting peacefully. "I don't know what to do."

I stared at her name for a little longer and shook myself off and stood. I placed my hand over the letters of her name before I broke. "I'm so sorry I couldn't save you, Addie." I walked away, unable to stay any longer. I rubbed my fingers across my check, wiping the wetness away. "Goodbye, Addie."

CHAPTER
Thirty-One

Charlie

$\mathcal{I}$ stood at the window, watching as Alex drove away. His shoulders were tense and he looked so angry. I knew it was probably with me. I knew he was most likely growing agitated with me for not speaking to him. I *wanted* to speak to him. I *wanted* to break in front of him and have him put me back together but I knew if I did that, he would see the ugly parts inside of me.

I was scared that if he saw the parts I wanted to hide from the world, he wouldn't want me anymore. I was scared that if he saw how selfish I was at being relieved that I was still here—me and my baby—that he would be just as disgusted with me as I was with myself.

I turned away and walked to the sofa. I placed my

hand on the armrest and used it to slowly lower myself down. This bump just seemed to be getting bigger by the day.

The door to the apartment slowly opened before James walked in. "Can I come in?" he asked.

"Of course." I gave him a smile, not needing another man to worry about me.

"I brought chocolate." He held it out to me, giving me a grin when I took it. "I left Scott downstairs so that we could hang out."

"You don't need to babysit me." I placed the bar on top of my bump, chuckling when it wobbled at the force of the baby's kick. "The company is nice, though."

He looked past me, his eyes going to the side. He was looking at the photo of Addie and me.

"I miss her," he whispered.

"Me too." I picked the bar of chocolate up and placed it on the arm of the sofa. "Every day."

"She wouldn't want this," he said, turning his gaze back to mine. "She wouldn't."

"Wouldn't want what?" I asked.

"This." He waved his hand at me. "You. Like this." He leaned forward, resting his elbows on his knees. "Can I show you something?"

"Sure." I nodded my head, curious about what he wanted to show me.

He got up and walked past me, disappearing into mine and Alex's bedroom.

What the hell was he doing?!

Before I could say anything, he was coming back and taking his seat opposite me. "I want you to know that I will get my fucking arse kicked by him when I show you this."

"What is it?" I asked. I was scared and confused. What could be so bad that would make Alex want to hide it from me? We shared everything. At least, I thought that we did.

"I understand," I whispered.

He stared at me a moment longer before he stood up and dipped his hand into his jeans pocket, tossing an item next to me.

I watched as it bounced on the sofa. I couldn't hide the shock that I was a feeling. It was a ring box. There was only one type of ring that he would want to keep hidden from me.

"He was going to propose to you before all of this happened." He looked at me with sympathy. "He, uh…" He hesitated, looking away from me.

"He what?" I asked. I needed to know what he wanted to say. I needed him to be honest with me.

"He thinks he's losing you." He linked his hands together, keeping his eyes on me. "He thinks you don't want to be here with him anymore. You don't seem happy for the little life that is about to join you."

"Don't say that!" I couldn't stop the tears leaking from my eyes. "I want to be here. I do." I looked away from him, wiping my face. "I just don't know how to do this." I choked back a sob, feeling my chest tighten. "I—I don't know how to do this without her." I was all but wailing, and I knew I was scaring him.

"Hey. Hey." He slid onto his knees in front of me, grasping my hands. "Calm down. It's okay." He rubbed his thumbs along my knuckles, reminding me so much of his brother.

"I love my baby. I do." He had to believe me. "I lost her!" I put my hand over my mouth, trying to stop the sobs. "I told her to go. I saw her fall and I…" I covered my face with my hands. "And I couldn't catch her in time!"

The cushions dipped next to me as James wrapped his arms around me and pulled me into his chest. He rocked us from side to side for a few minutes, trying to comfort me.

My tears slowly dried and the sobs eased. His rocking was lulling me into a calmness. "I can't lose him, James," I whispered. "I lost Addie and I can't lose Alex."

He rested his chin on top of my head before I felt his chest move. "We need to do better, Charlie." Now he sounded sad. "I've been okay-ish in the day but sometimes, in the night, I struggle." He rested his cheek against my hair. "She wouldn't want this, though, Charlie. She wouldn't want us struggling to go on."

"I know." I rested my hand on his chest,

appreciating him more in that moment than I thought was possible.

"She was a hero. She gave her life for you and that little one." He gently tapped my stomach. "We need to go on and show her what she gave her life for." He looked down at me, drawing my gaze. "We need to find a way to live our lives as though she were still with us."

I nodded my head and rested it back in its spot on his chest. Several moments of silence passed before I spoke again.

"I love you, James." I didn't expect a response but of course I got one.

"I know." He sounded a little cocky and it made me chuckle.

We rested there for several more moments before we were disturbed by the door opening behind us.

"Hey. What's going on?" Alex stood at the door, giving us a small smile.

It was a fake smile. It didn't reach his eyes and it didn't set me aflame like his smiles normally did.

"Nothing, man. Just hanging out." He patted my hand that was resting on my bump as he stood up. He widened his eyes at me and sneakily handed me the ring box before he walked towards Alex. "Take it easy on her, man," he whispered. He patted him on the shoulder before he slipped past him, out the door.

"Hi." I looked over at him, hating how exhausted he looked. It hadn't been easy on him. I stretched my arm out to him, beckoning him closer. "Come and sit with me." I placed the ring box in the pocket of my cardigan.

He came over and took the seat that James had vacated. "You've been crying." He reached over and stroked his thumb beneath my eye.

"Yes." I looked down before turning my body to face him a little. I grabbed his hand and placed it over my bump. "I'm sorry I've been difficult."

"You haven't been difficult," he said, shaking his head. "You have been grieving."

"I've been lost," I whispered, finally admitting the truth. "Since she left, she… I…"

"She didn't leave you, darling."

"I know." I nodded my head, trying to agree. "I know that she didn't mean to leave, but it feels like she left me." I wiped the tears from my cheeks. "I'm having a baby and it's scary and…" I could feel a sob building. "I needed my best friend to go through this with me and she's not here…"

"You have me," he whispered. His eyes reflected tears back at me before he began to rub his thumb along the back of my hand.

"I know."

"I went to see her today," he admitted.

"Addie?" I looked at him in shock. "You went to her grave?"

"Yeah." He gave me a crooked smile. "I took roses for her."

"Alex." I was an emotional wreck to begin with, but picturing him taking her flowers and talking to her… It killed me inside.

"I needed someone to talk to. Someone who loves you just as much as I do."

I reached over and stroked my thumb along his cheekbone. "It means a lot that you went there."

"I owe her everything, Charlie. She saved my reason for living." He sniffed, shaking his head to clear it. "I'll be grateful to her until the day that I die for her sacrifice."

I took his hands and brought them back to my bump. "Maybe she's still with us," I whispered.

We both looked down at my bump before meeting each other's eyes. A smile passed between us and I knew we were both imagining a little girl.

"Maybe," he whispered. "How was James?" he asked, his eyes drifting to the closed door of his apartment.

"He'll be okay," I whispered. "He told me that we need to live for her."

His chocolate brown eyes gazed into mine.

"He also showed me something," I whispered.

He frowned at me for a second before he spoke. "What did he show you?"

"This." I pulled my hand away and dipped it into

the pocket of my cardigan. I grabbed the box and reached over, placing it into his open palm.

He looked at it in shock before he looked back up to my eyes. "Uh…" He chuckled. "Wow, this isn't how I imagined doing it."

We both laughed at his words before I spoke. "Then do it how you imagined doing it."

"You're not ready." He shook his head at me. "You need time and I —"

"The one thing I have learned, Alex," I said, interrupting him, "is that time is the one thing we don't have." I shook my head sadly. "Addie was twenty-seven years old. What does that say about time? We have one life, and I think it is time that we started living it. For you. For me. For Addie and for whatever special person is growing inside of me."

"You're serious." He looked so surprised at my words.

"I am." I stroked my fingers down the side of his face. "It's like James said: we need to start living and give Addie happy moments to look down at."

He nodded before he slid off the sofa and fell down on one knee. "Miss Charlotte Chase." He reached for my hand, squeezing my fingers. "I promise to love, cherish and adore you until the day I die. I will be here for all the scary moments and all of the happy ones. I have waited a long time for you, and I want to spend the rest of my life loving you and only you." He smiled at me, a full, megawatt, beaming smile. "Charlie, will you do me the honour of being the love of my life, my soulmate, my wife?" He opened the box and I gasped as the beautiful diamond stone twinkled up at me. His words were beautiful, but as I saw his hand shake, I knew his nerves were most likely all tangled up inside.

"Yes," I whispered. "Yes!" I held my hand out for him, laughing when his head slumped back on his shoulders in extreme relief.

He slid the ring on to my finger where it fit perfectly before he leaned forward and pressed his lips to mine. He took the seat back at my side and placed his arm around my shoulders, pulling me in to his side.

"I'm glad that's over."

I giggled at his words before turning my head and looking up at him. "Did you think I would say no?" I asked, curious now more than ever.

He looked down at me before his fingers began stroking patterns over my arm. "I didn't know." He dipped his head and kissed my lips. "Fate hasn't really been on our side lately, has she?"

"No, I guess not." I rubbed my stomach where our little one was kicking. "Maybe that'll change now." I cuddled closer to him. "Maybe our darkest days are behind us." I closed my eyes, imagining Addie as our own personal guardian angel. I was sure that if she was in heaven, she'd send only good things for us from now on.

CHAPTER
Thirty-Two

Alex

It had been several weeks since I'd popped the question and made Charlie my fiancé. Since then, things had gotten a little easier. They weren't perfect, and I didn't think they ever would be. At the end of the day, life wasn't perfect. It was supposed to be hard, but we were making the best of it.

Charlie was due to give birth in a week's time, and to say I was tense would be an understatement. Every time she moved, I thought it was coming. I spent my evenings upstairs with her in our apartment and she spent some of her days down here on the comfy sofa by the window.

We had both taken on additional staff. The café was doing so well and the further along her pregnancy got, the less baking she had done until she stopped baking altogether and had been using suppliers for everything. She hated doing it, but the café certainly didn't suffer from it. She had a strong customer base, and I knew her regulars were eager for her to return back to work when she was ready.

James and Addie had planned a baby shower and we all decided to cancel it. Charlie didn't want it without Addie and I couldn't really blame her.

"Sweetie." She came around the bar, holding the bottom of her back.

"How is the back?" I asked. "Take a seat and I'll bring you a cup of tea over." She had taken a huge liking for fruity tea in the last few weeks. I thought it was disgusting but she insisted that it relaxed her.

"Alex." She gave me a smile and it was easy to see that she was glowing. "We need to go."

"Go?" I asked. "Where are we going? What are…?" I looked at her and that was when I saw she was holding the bottom of her bump. "Oh, shit! Is the baby coming?" I shouted.

She laughed at my theatrics. "Yes. My water broke upstairs." She turned around to face the door as I went running past her. "Get my bag at the bottom of the stairs."

I was relieved when I saw James walking towards me with the bag in hand.

"Relax," he mouthed at me. "I'll drive. Let's go."

He gave Scott behind the bar a quick wave. "Look after the place, Scott. We'll be back with a little person."

Charlie giggled at how blasé he was. How could *they* be so calm? She was going to be squeezing a person out of her and she was acting like she was just popping next door for a coffee.

"Alex, sweetheart." She placed her hand on my shoulder. "What did we talk about? Don't panic."

"Right." I took a deep breath, trying to calm myself. "Don't panic," I muttered beneath my breath. "Panic later." I rushed ahead of her and held her door open, helping her into the passenger seat.

James climbed into the driver seat while I climbed into the back. "Let's go and meet this baby, then!" he said before he pulled out of his spot and drove us to the hospital, breaking a few too many speed limits on the way.

$\mathcal{W}$e had been at the hospital for a few hours now and there was still no baby. Her contractions had started about an hour ago and they were only getting worse. Charlie was handling it like a pro, though. She didn't swear too much, but whenever she gripped my hand, it was tighter than the time before.

"Why is this taking so long?" I asked, stupidly.

She rested her head back against the pillow behind her. "It's not like cooking a chicken." She chuckled at me. "This baby will come whenever the time is right."

"I'm sorry." I squeezed her hand before bringing it to my lips. "I don't like seeing you in pain."

"Me, neither," she quickly agreed.

Before I could say anything else, we were disturbed by a doctor coming into the room. "Okay, then, Miss Chase." He washed his hands at the sink before drying them and snapping on a pair of gloves. "Let's see if this baby is ready to come, shall we?"

I took a deep breath before sweeping her hair back that was sticking to her forehead. He placed himself between her legs and I knew that whatever was about to happen was going to change our lives forever.

She winced as he prodded her before he nodded to the nurse at his side.

"She's ready." He smiled up at us. I knew it was something he had likely done a hundred times before, but I still felt a thrill of terror shoot through me." "Okay, Charlie. When I say 'push', I need you to push for me. Okay?"

"Okay." She nodded her head before tightening her grip on my hand. "Let's do this."

J had watched many births on YouTube and had grossed myself out completely, but when the time came for my own child, I wanted to know what was going on. I didn't want any surprises. The biggest surprise in my own child's birth was how quick the baby came. Charlie had been pushing for a while, but the next command from the midwife's mouth ramped up the intensity of the room.

"Okay, Charlie. One more big push is all I need you to do."

She blew out a deep breath before she lifted herself up onto her pillows. She was soaked through with sweat, and her hospital gown was sticking to her. She squeezed my hand as she gave one final push before she slumped back against the pillows, her chest heaving with pain and exertion.

Seconds later, we heard the most beautiful sound in the whole world. The cries of our child.

"Charlie. Alex." The midwife held her arms up, showing us our baby. "You have a baby girl."

Charlie collapsed into sobs, tightening her hand in mine.

"A baby girl!" I turned my face to hers and kissed her lips, resting our foreheads against each other. "You did so good, darling. So damn good!"

"Can I hold her?" she asked.

"Yes, sweetheart. I'll have to take her to get cleaned

up but here you go." She gently placed our baby in Charlie's arms.

I could feel the tears running down my face. I knew how precious this moment was and there wasn't anything more perfect or beautiful than the sight of my woman and baby girl embracing for the first time.

Charlie looked up at me, her glossy eyes brimming with emotion. "You're a daddy!" she enthused.

"Yeah." I reached down, loving the dark head of hair that our little girl had. "She's so beautiful." I bent my head and pressed my lips to Charlie's, pouring all of my love for her into that kiss. "Just like her mummy."

The nurse took our baby away to get her cleaned up and weighed. They moved Charlie to the ward after they'd cleaned her up and changed her into a fresh gown and I went to collect James.

He shot to his feet when he saw me. "What did she have?" he asked. He held his hands out, waiting.

"You have a niece!" I grinned at him, loving how happy he looked in this moment.

"Yes!" He slammed his body against mine, hugging me tightly before roughly slapping his hand against my back. "I'm so fucking proud of you!"

"Come and meet her," I offered. I led him back to Charlie's room, smiling at the sight that greeted me. We both took a spot on either side of her bed, all looking down in awe at the beautiful new soul in the world.

"What's her name?" James asked.

Charlie looked up at me, gazing at me with a twinkle in her eyes. I knew what she was asking without her needing to say anything. I nodded my head, agreeing with her completely in that moment.

"This is Addison Charlotte Winters," she said. "Addison, this is your uncle James."

It was impossible for James to stop the tears from rolling down his cheeks. "Hi, Addison." He reached out and stroked the knuckle of his finger over her cheek. "I'm your uncle and I'm going to spoil you rotten."

We all gasped as she turned her face to James's hand.

"Welcome back to the world, Addie," Charlie whispered before she bent her head and pressed the softest kiss to her forehead.

Epilogue

Charlie

It had been two years since little Addison had been born. Two years and three months since our world had changed for the better. Just like her namesake, little Addison was a terror on legs. She was into everything and could never sit still for longer than five minutes.

Today was the day that I would become Charlotte Winters, and to say I was nervous would be an understatement. It was the first day I hadn't seen Addison in the morning, and I was missing her a little. Her daddy had decided she would spend the morning with him while I got ready.

We had booked rooms at The Savoy Hotel in the

centre of London. Alex had insisted that we would only ever be doing this once and that every woman should be a princess on her wedding day.

My mum had come down from Wales and she would be responsible for Addison during our wedding. James would be standing up with Alex and me as we said our vows as Alex's best man. I had decided not to have a maid of honour or any bridesmaids. I knew that Addie would be with me in spirit.

I stared at my reflection, willing the tears back. I couldn't cry. Not today. Today was for happiness only.

"Knock, knock," a voice called from the door.

"James!" I turned to face him before standing. I gave him a little twirl. "What do you think?"

My bridal dress was sleeveless and it fanned out from the knees down. It was very lacy and it had a belt of daisies around the waist. It was very simple. I'd made sure Addison had a matching dress but hers had sleeves and was a lot frillier.

"Wow!" He stepped forwards and pulled me into a hug. He kissed my cheek as he stepped back. "You look so beautiful, Charlie."

"Thank you." I smiled up at him, touched by his compliment. "How is the groom doing?"

He rolled his eyes. "Stressed. Addison is keeping him busy, though."

"How does she look?" I asked.

"Beautiful. As always." He reached over and tucked a curl behind my ear. "Just like her mum."

"Alex sent you to check on me, didn't he?" I asked.

"He's winding me up." He moved past me, taking a seat on a chair. "I can't take the pacing." He picked up my bouquet, admiring the daisies before placing it back down on the table. "I also came back here to give you a present."

"A present?" I grinned at him. "For me? Really?"

"Not that you deserve it," he said while rolling his eyes. "But, I thought you could use it today." He nodded his head to the chair next to him, gesturing for me to take a seat.

"What is it?" I asked. I took the seat and turned my body to face him.

He reached into his pocket and pulled something out. He kept his fist closed, hiding it for a moment before he moved his fingers, the item dangling between us.

I gasped when I saw Addie's chain bracelet. It had all her charms still on it, and I knew how much he treasured this piece of jewellery. It was the only thing of Addie's that he still had as her mother had taken all of her belongings back to Manchester with her.

"James," I whispered, awestruck.

"I know she's here with you," he said quietly. He sounded choked up, and I knew he was just as emotional about this bracelet as I was. "But I thought..." He reached over and fastened it over my pulse-point. "By wearing a little piece of her, she could be with you physically."

This time, I couldn't stop the tears from trailing over my cheeks. "I miss her so much," I whispered.

"I know you do." He reached over and wiped the tears off my cheek with his thumb. "I keep thinking it'll get easier but she's hard to move on from."

I reached up and slid my arms around his shoulders, hugging him tightly.

He rocked us gently from side to side gently, squeezing me before letting go.

"I also came to your room for another purpose." He reached down and took my hands. "As your mother is looking after princess, I was wondering if I could have the pleasure of giving you away."

I looked at him in surprise, touched again by how beautiful this man was. Inside and out.

"I would love that," I whispered.

---

*a*fter making myself presentable, we made our way downstairs. Standing outside the hall where we would say our vows, my hands began to shake.

"Nervous?" James grinned at me.

"Yes." I laughed. "I'm about to become Mrs. Winters."

The opening notes of the wedding march began from behind the doors seconds before they opened. We'd kept it small, wanting this day to be private. The girls that Addie had worked with were here and some of Alex's friends, including his friend from prison, Anton. I was surprised but I think he thought a lot more of Alex than he ever cared to admit.

James took my arm as we slowly began our walk down the aisle. We both laughed when we saw Addison waving theatrically at us as we passed her. I reached out, stroking her hair as we passed. She had a headband of daisies on her head and she looked so beautiful in her dress.

James turned to shake Alex's hand and pulled him into a hug before he stepped aside.

"You look so beautiful, darling." Alex took my hand and pulled it to his lips as we turned to face the registrar.

He gave us a polite smile before he placed his hand on the prayer book in his hand. "Are you ready to be joined in holy matrimony?" he asked.

We both turned to look at each other and smiled.

"Yes," I whispered.

We went for the traditional vows, not wanting anything extravagant. We just wanted to be husband

and wife, a family and to spend the rest of our lives together.

As we exchanged rings, I smiled when Alex rubbed his thumb over my wrist where Addie's bracelet was displayed. His eyes glistened at me, and I knew in that moment that Addie wasn't just with James and me: she was with us all.

"I now pronounce you man and wife," the registrar said. "Alex, you may kiss your bride."

He placed his finger beneath my chin and tilted my face before he dipped his head and pressed his lips softly to mine. "I love you," he whispered.

"Forever." I gave him a beaming smile, loving him completely in that moment.

We turned to face our guests as they stood up to give us a clap. I gazed at my mum, loving how happy she looked as she watched us. I watched her stand before placing Addison down on her feet.

She toddled over to us, her arms outstretched. Alex bent down and scooped her into his arms. He held her against his hip as he wrapped his other arm around my shoulders and held me to him. He bent his head and kissed our daughter's cheek before he did the same to mine.

We walked down the aisle and made our way outside to where there was an old-fashioned Rolls Royce idling at the kerb. The three of us climbed in, securing Addison between us.

"Are you happy?" Alex asked.

I looked up at him, able to answer that question honestly for the first time since Addison's death. "I am." I reached over and kissed his lips. "We're a family." I reached down and stroked the hair on top of Addison's head. "Forever and always."

Acknowledgements

A big thank you to my beta team. Your enthusiasm for this story has been amazing and I love how excited you have all been for these characters. Wendy, Jayne, Laura, Lorren, Tracey, Paula and Emma. You girlies rock!

To my editor and cover designer, Eleanor. Thank you for making such beautiful covers and for being so fabulous to work with.

To my models, Lance and Cassia. Thank you so much for bringing my characters to life!

To my sprint team – Sienna, Stacy, Alice, Heather and Adina. Thank you doesn't seem enough but I am grateful for all of your words of encouragement and support in making sure I hit my daily word goals.

To my partners in crime, Carmel and Scarlet. Your support has been amazing!

To Susan, my mum. Thank you for being so strong! I'm proud of how far you have come.

Lastly, to the readers. Thank you for taking a chance on this indie author and I hope you love reading this book as much as I did writing it.

Remember, reviews are awesome so if you could leave me a review on Amazon, Goodreads or Bookbub, I would be so grateful.

Also by
Lizzie James

Tangled Series

Tangled Web

Tangled Lies

Tangled Truths

Tangled Pieces

Kindred Series

Missing Piece

Perfect Fit

Rough Love

Printed in Great Britain
by Amazon

26576368R10185